THE REFUGE

BOOK ONE OF THE REFUGE TRILOGY

THE REFUGE

N. FORD

atmosphere press

A wind harp is a harp constructed outside so as the winds blow, heaven's music plays. On a pleasant day, breezes caress the wind harp's strings, floating the air with light melodies. During a storm, however, winds push against the harp and through the violence, rises a triumphant song - one which climbs above the noise of the fight.

I am simple strings stretched across a solid place.
The Sender of the winds - He's a masterful composer.

This story, and every one that follows, are created by Him, through Him, and for Him.

Soli deo gloria.

PROLOGUE

The Physis Sea

Jude walked the deck as he did every morning, the ship so much a part of him it extended from his every limb. No matter the tide, his steps knew how to meet the deck. The ocean lived in his veins and carried his chest up and down, a breath with every wave.

He worked his list instinctively, checking the lay of each cracked board; the wear of every old rope; and the drape of each tattered mast. She was old, and she moaned against every nudge of a wave; but she was his, and as reliable as the day her dry boards met water.

Jude scanned a glowing horizon. Empty of foreign sails and blanketed with the morning pink of sunlit, cotton clouds, he moved on to mark off the crewmen dutifully filling every post. Some waved. Others nodded. Some wiped away sweat and then tipped a hat to their captain. Each had a unique reason for being there—for spending their hours on his ship—but the reasons didn't matter much to Jude. What mattered was that they were fully dedicated to the mission, and that's why it worked.

Jude executed his routine as normally as ever but couldn't shake the thought that it felt more important than ever before. The urgency in him grew ever harder to suppress, so he turned his mind to task, hoping to *seem* composed at the very least.

It felt as if he'd lived lifetimes in the two years they'd been away. Proof of it etched permanently into the creases around his eyes. It was nothing like he'd thought it would be. Thoughts badgered him about what it would have been like if they'd never left, mocking his reach for a life that might somehow matter... but wondering about what might have been was not productive. He pushed away unrelenting hypotheticals and forced his mind back to the work at hand.

Jude took inventory, counting and recounting every sheet, gauze, and medicine vial. Satisfied, he moved above deck to watch the sun climb above the eastern sea. It was time to return. The journey would be long—a few months at its most expeditious flight. And it would be dangerous—although not any more so than any other since they'd left.

The choice they'd made to fly no color of allegiance was a risk, and the weight of that choice sat heavily inside him. Neutrality came with a cost. But the cost seemed much higher now, and it yanked him from the original mission and redirected his most urgent attentions to returning.

Determination stirred in his belly and overcame his presence as he approached the man at the helm—a man so close a friend he called him 'brother.'

"East, Jonathan," Jude said.

Jonathan raised an eyebrow but nothing else. His response asked the question without asking it.

Jude squinted, tightening the muscles around his eyes, and with an exhale and the slightest dip of his chin, he responded, "Zoar."

The look on Jude's face offered the only explanation Jonathan needed and with a jerk of the wheel, the Refuge took its oldest and most familiar course—that of home.

CHAPTER ONE

MAE

Zoar

Steam rattled against the tea pot, drumming it with discontent. Mae rhythmically responded to its readiness in well-practiced routine. She poured hot water into a waiting mug and inhaled deeply over its warmth. She padded across her creaking home's floor to a rickety screen door that opened to a charactered, wood-paneled porch. The painted white wood cracked in places and peeled back in complaint against years of weather and wear. It bit at her bare feet in places, but she didn't mind. It was everything they'd dreamed it would be. She only wished he was here to enjoy it with her.

The morning orange of the sun broke over a watery horizon and shot rays through clouds like a crown. No morning looked the same. Some were brilliantly blazoned with colors that couldn't be recreated at the grandest of efforts. Others were blanketed in grey, casting a dullness over their vibrant island in odd, faded shadows and blurred outlines. But one thing held common through each morning's cloth or cotton was the newness each one wore, like mercy and light married together in victory—whether brilliant or bland—defiant victory still. And Mae clung to each one afresh, every morning.

She moved to the edge of the porch and bent carefully over a protesting railing. The wood creaked, even beneath her slight frame, and her eyes searched to find her friend. Sarah was found quickly, sitting on her rocking chair, pushing back and forth in time with the tide, watching the same brilliant ascent of the sun Mae did. Sarah's house sat just down the hill from Mae's—just as they'd planned it. Mae didn't have to peer over the railing to know Sarah would be there, but checking each day carried a comfort with it she was unwilling to release. Comforts were not egregious in their offerings, and Mae was determined to capture each flicker and hold it tenderly—even if it was the simple sight of her dearest friend.

Mae reentered her kitchen to set the table. It wouldn't be long before Sarah would ascend the hill to join her. Though each had lost her husband long ago, they'd found a rich and enduring friendship in each other. The joy and battle of raising their boys together only bound them tighter. And now, the boys had been gone for what felt like an eternity.

At the beginning, she and Sarah wondered together about what the boys might experience, or what adventures they may have encountered along the way. But after a year, their mothers' wonderings faded and the reality of their labored wait set in. It felt much easier to discuss the children at school, or the latest news from council, or the gossip making its way around the island than it did to wonder about the safety, adventure, or defeat the boys may be experiencing.

"How long?" she wondered out loud to an empty room.

How long would they wait until their sons returned?

In the absence of an answer, Mae took a place at her table, inhaled over steam, and waited.

TWENTY YEARS EARLIER

Sleeves up at the school and herding an ever-growing number of children, Mae wrangled toddlers who were due for morning naps. She looked around the busy room. They would hit capacity soon—again. The war was producing more orphans than they would be able to manage without more space and more help. In ways, she was thankful for her empty womb. There were far too many parent-less children already.

She heard the bells clang the arrival of a new shipment of refugees but hadn't the time to go. Bombings of unprotected territories and war on civilian grounds created refugees by the ship full. If there were unclaimed children in the arrival, someone would bring them. The school was the only place for them to go.

Sarah approached with a child on her hip and another holding her free hand. "Do you want me to go?" she asked.

Mae shook her head. "They know where we are."

"I can send Jonathan," Sarah offered, waving him over.

"Let him be, Sarah," Mae said.

Mae wanted to protect the boy's childhood for as long as possible. Physis was unforgiving in so many ways. The boy didn't need to see the trauma of war on refugees' faces just yet.

"I can help," Jonathan said. "What can I do?"

Mae placed a tender hand under his chin. His seven-year-old frame was already brutish. He would look like a man long before he would turn into one.

"Baby, run down to the docks and bring the orphans up to us," Sarah instructed.

Jonathan nodded understanding at his mother's instructions and left through the big red door in the back of the schoolhouse. He was quiet and compliant and uncomplaining.

"He's marvelous," Mae said, watching him go.

"He ought to be," Sarah quipped. "He's got you and me for parents." She smiled wryly while Mae laughed.

Thankful for the levity, Mae tucked another little one in with the other toddlers. He was the fifth and last child who would fit in the crib made for one.

"We're going to need another," Mae said, resting over the crib's wooden bed frame.

"Add it to the list for the carpenter," Sarah replied hopelessly.

They both knew the list was already tired with absent necessities and a crib added to the list would be nothing more than a sugared fantasy, but Mae scribbled it down anyway.

Mae wiped the back of a hand against her glistening forehead and placed a hand on each hip to prioritize what would need to happen next. Toddlers lay cozied in for their naps. Infants were in various states of being changed or fed. Older children worked with the few staff they had to spare on reading or writing. Not an inch of the schoolhouse was unused, and children outnumbered adults twenty to one. Mae wondered how long they could keep this pace and survive. At some point, the children would suffer more for the school's lack of resources, but the war would rage on disregarding the island's needs. The war didn't see people. It only recognized power.

As Mae considered the state of the school and its future, the big red door in the back of the schoolhouse cracked open again, slowly, pouring morning sun into the room in streams that awoke the cells in Mae's flesh.

"Mama?"

Jonathan's small, sweet voice rang squeakier than normal, dressed in uncommon unsteadiness for the stalwart boy. A small, dark boy clung to one of Jonathan's legs, causing him to shuffle forward in uncoordinated pitches, unbalanced and unsure of what to do with the package he'd acquired.

The small boy's eyes were big and dark, and they stopped when they found Mae. From twitch to contentment, they settled there, and though child chatter filled the spaces around her, the world went silent and fell still all at once.

Sarah spoke the only words Mae heard.

"Your son."

PRESENT DAY

Mae smiled at the memory, reflecting on Sarah's sure words and the profoundness of simplicity when unquestionable, irrevocable, destiny is spoken into clear air.

Jude was meant for her all along. He didn't come from her. They didn't match like Physis dictated they should. But he was hers. And she thought, when he left, it would be hardest thing she ever did to let him go.

But waiting for Jude and Jonathan to return surpassed that ache long ago.

Mae's thoughts were interrupted by the creak and smack of the screen door on her back porch.

"Good, you're here," Mae said. "Let's ea—"

Mae's words cut short at the sight of her friend. Sarah's skin shined with uncommon perspiration and her usual bronzy glow yellowed into a paled haze.

"Sarah?" Mae asked.

Sarah took only one step inside the house and crumbled to the floor at Mae's feet.

CHAPTER TWO

MATTHEW

The Diamond Isles

Matthew stood in front of the ornate mirror that decorated his bedchamber's largest wall. His hands gripped at both its sides blending his white knuckles into his pale skin. He tried to relieve the angst in his neck by pushing on the unforgiving knots that collected there. He worked around the three diamonds embedded into the base of his skull. They were the universal sign of Diamond Isles royalty and without doubt, the primary cause of the stress he tried so unsuccessfully to quiet.

Matthew searched the reflection that looked back at him and begged it for a sign of life. Dead pools of blue stared back at him. Silence hung in the space between his face and his reflection. The only thing that moved in the expansive room around him was his own breath. He hated that about this room. It was so large even the smallest noise reverberated across the marble floors and walls and floated up its sides to taunt him from the stupidly high ceiling above him. Nothing could live unheard here—not even death. He moved across the empty space and pushed open the double doors to his balcony, letting the cold spill into the expanse that surrounded him. At least the sound of the sea could still drown out the silence—and he was counting on it.

A knock at the door forced him out of his trance while a blushing housemaid hesitatingly peeked around the opulent oak door at the front of his bedchamber.

"Pardon, your majesty. Dinner is served."

He offered her a slight smile, feeling sorry for her obvious response to him, but he was used to it. Female company always acted foolishly in his presence—housemaid or otherwise—but it was the quiet ones who turned red upon eye contact that made him soften. He was the only child of the king and queen of the Diamond Isles, and that fact alone made him the most desired man in the eons of sea that surrounded them. His pure features, symmetrical face, and fountained inheritance only added to the prize.

"Hello darling."

His mother greeted him from her wheelchair at the end of the table. She'd been sick for years, but only in the last few months had she taken to a wheelchair. He still wasn't used to it. Seeing his beloved mother withering away was more than he could bear most days. Trying his best to disguise his discomfort at the sight, he bent awkwardly to kiss her and took his place in the middle of the table.

His father cleared his throat before speaking to him. "Matthew, am I to understand that you denied yet another meeting with a possible match for this evening?"

Matthew smiled at the housemaid who was delicately placing his first course before him, unmoved by the thrill it gave her.

"Father, I decided to spend the evening studying the books. You're always saying how diligently I must learn to rule before taking over as king, so tonight I will put myself to the task of learning for the sake of our great kingdom."

Matthew knew he delivered the last part with a little too much sarcasm, but he let himself grin into it anyway.

His father started in on the long-abused lecture of the necessity of choosing a successful and suitable match, but the queen mercifully cut the king off.

"Darling, must we talk so soon about Matthew's match? Let us not ruin our meal so early, hmm?" She waved a hand slightly over her plate and smiled at the king sweetly. "There must be something else we can discuss for a while."

Matthew loved that his mother was still willing to use her wifely power to win him a few moments of peace. He discreetly winked his thanks at her and welcomed the tiniest breath of relief with a bite.

The king softened immediately. She'd always been able to do that. Sometimes Matthew wasn't sure how the marriage between them worked after all these years, but it did. Matthew didn't know if the king loved anything in his life apart from the queen. He'd often wondered if his father even ever loved him. He wondered if the king simply put up with him because he had to—maybe even because the queen made him. To Matthew, his mother had always defended the king, touting a good man under all the guise of tyrannical rule, but Matthew wasn't persuaded. Studying under his father the last few years, Matthew questioned many of the choices his father made, and those of the rulers before him. The more he learned, the more he questioned. Hundreds of years of Diamond Isles rulers had followed the same philosophies as his father, and they remained the singular authority in Physis. This kind of rule had made them what they were—strong. And it made them rich. Most importantly, it made them a name no other territory in Physis would question. But Matthew did.

"Very well," surrendered the king. "I have additional news anyway."

The queen raised her eyebrows while she ate, inviting him to continue with a wave of her fork.

The king turned slightly toward Matthew with an arrogant grin. "Tomorrow, son, you've your first visit to Triton."

Matthew exhaled sharply, losing his appetite with his breath. He'd been dreading this visit for years. The royal family was not a welcome sight in Triton. In fact, they were hardly tolerated. Any pure brave enough to show his or her face in Triton would be equal parts resented and envied. The stories of pures being attacked, hit with rocks, or having food thrown at them haunted Matthew since his childhood. Having grown in the palace of the Diamond Isles, a place where he was nearly worshiped, it was hard to picture a world in which the opposite was true—both outcomes the result of mere genetics. It had perplexed him for the length of his memory.

The historical separation of pure from tainted was always more than a division of physical traits. The Diamond Isles were made up of a mountainous string of islands rich with diamond resources. The very soil sparkled with their abundance and the cliffs that made up its seaside shimmered for miles across the coast, witnessed by approaching ships long before their arrival. Luxurious estates built high atop the mountains crowned them a glory to match. Pure families with unadulterated blood lines wore the trademark blue and white features that marked them as Diamond Isles royalty. The priority of the day was the arrangement of advantageous marriages, matched to keep pure blood lines pure, and to ensure the continued separation of pure from tainted. What Matthew was learning more every day, was that the separation wasn't about genetics at all. It was about resources.

He'd never seen Triton, but he may as well have. The evidence of what he would witness was written in the books he studied day after day. He knew the contrast well. Triton was a mining territory. It contained squared barracks occupied only by night. Triton citizens not assigned to fight in the war were assigned to mine—most often sorted and assigned by physical ability and nothing else. Non-respecting of gender or age, man, woman, and child were syphoned to work by their ability, administered by the Diamond Isles authorities that ran Triton's operations. One may live in Triton; but it was under no illusion. Living on Triton meant working to prosper the isles. It wasn't a choice. It was a birthright. On the isles, the birthright was that of abundance. On Triton, birthright was servitude. Those assigned to the war fought a fight they hadn't started and from which they would not profit.

It wasn't hard for Matthew to understand why a culture of detestation thrived there. If that's what awaited him tomorrow, he wasn't going to waste another minute sitting at the dinner table. He'd lost his appetite at his father's first words anyway.

Matthew pushed away from a full plate and angled his body toward the king, his eyes locking onto the nothingness that littered the air between them.

"If you'll excuse me," he managed.

He bowed slightly to each of his parents and left for his bedchamber. The silence of the room that had tortured him only a short while before, now offered a reprieve he welcomed. With emotion leaking down into his fists, Matthew strode through the empty room and out to the balcony where he gripped the railing affixed atop a sparkling diamond cliff. He stared down into the angry waves below him and let the sound of their smashing fill his ears.

They would make the only good company he would find tonight.

CHAPTER THREE

JUDE

The Physis Sea

As the setting sun melted into a hazy horizon, Jude stood on the deck of the Refuge, a fixture of its very design. He remembered the days leading up to his departure from Zoar when he'd strained for direction—for a call. Now he felt as if he'd trade anything for silence from it.

Once attained, the call moved about him as a ghost, haunting his every choice, monitoring his every moment, hovering over his every thought. Was he now choosing to abandon the purpose he'd begged for only a few years prior? Was he a coward to pursue the safety Zoar offered? Was the growing urgency inside him driven only by the fear of losing what he loved most?

Jude fought to reconcile the thoughts that peppered his consciousness. He watched as the orange sky faded to match the blue of the sea and wondered how he could maintain his honor while he left the war and the wounded behind him.

He wondered if he would ever return. He didn't know that

purpose had the potential to grow a life of its own and reprioritize itself independent of him. But it did. In the blink of an eye, it did. The wood of the ship creaked below him against the waves and sung to him a lullaby he knew he was made to hear. It comforted him in a way nothing else could.

The cool of the evening sea breeze blew steadily into his face while he contemplated the new exigencies in front of him. He had to think of Collette. Her safety and preservation were more important than anything. Now the life that grew inside her consumed Jude's every thought. What used to be the daily charge to keep safe the ship and crew had become, in one moment, a non-negotiable, no-fail mission more critical than anything Jude had ever known.

He must return Collette to Zoar.

Collette approached from behind him, "brooding, as Mae would say, is unbecoming."

Jude smiled at Collette's words without turning around to meet them.

"She'll be happy to know you quote her as often as you do," he replied.

He felt Collette's arms wrap around him from behind. He loved that, and he smiled into the space in front of him and then turned to face her.

"And soon, my love, soon you will be able to tell her yourself." She smiled at him. "You must be so happy at the thought of seeing her."

"I am," his smile faded as he said it.

"What?" Collette asked.

He was silent for a moment and shook his head gently. "Nothing."

She waited.

Jude knew he would lose, as he always did with Collette. He let his eyes fall to the ground before forcing them back up to meet hers.

"I was just remembering leaving," he admitted.

He smiled weakly and his voice drifted into the space in between them. The images of their departure ran across his recollection...

ZOAR
TWO YEARS EARLIER

Crystal clear water lapped the side of the skiff that hungrily awaited its passengers. The Refuge floated in the center of the bay, framing the scene behind them while simultaneously fueling the life that awaited them. Families of the ragtag crew from the Heap, one of Zoar's more colloquial names, scattered the white beaches of the Western Bay in bundles of desperate clutches.

Some found the mission honorable. Some thought it was nothing more than the hopeless efforts of a naïve dreamer.

Jude figured they were both right. Whichever was closer to the truth didn't matter because it didn't take knowing to light the fire.

Three perpetual loners had raised quick hands to join a cause. Maybe because they had nothing to do or nowhere to go. Maybe they, like Jude, sought some sort of purpose for their lives. This could be it for them, and just the chance for meaning was enough to sign them up.

Others who had joined the cause were recruited because the Refuge crew needed skills—deck hands, navigators, and one of the only chefs on the island. They were necessary additions to the mission.

Jude was especially thankful to have Chef Jackson join them. He was a constant fixture and friend in Zoar. Chef Jackson was someone, like many in Zoar, who the rest of the territories referred to as altered, or worse, mutated. He'd been born with what was considered a deformation and was exiled to the Heap shortly after his birth. It was common for those who existed in Zoar. It's what gave the island its name, the Heap. It was the place in Physis that took the other territories' throwaways.

To the crew of the Refuge, Chef Jackson was a delight, a source of joy, and most importantly, an adept chef. On the seas of Physis, however, Chef Jackson would be nothing more than a mutant. His well-being, along with any other obviously fallible crew member, would be at great risk. They had all joined willingly, knowing their safety would be in question from the moment they pulled anchor. But it hadn't stopped them from wanting to do something that mattered. And Jude wasn't going to turn them away if they wanted to help. He knew intimately the need to feel like he was contributing, and he wasn't going to withhold that from anyone, for any reason.

Rounding out the crew were people Jude considered to be like himself. They were dreamers, believing they could make Physis better than what the last 150 years had offered its inhabitants. Among them were Collette and Jonathan—his new wife, and his best friend—neither of whom would have let him do it without them.

He remembered standing with Jonathan before pushing off in the skiff. They'd stood with their backs to the Refuge and their faces turned directly upon the two women who had raised them—and from whom they'd never been more than the island's diameter away. The idea of leaving them tossed Jude's stomach in unrelenting circles. He remembered standing there, torn between a clear call on his life, and the sentiment of the sacrifice of what had made him able to do it in the first place—the love of a mother.

While struggling against his emotions, Mae rose through the strain first, as she always did. She smiled at him through silent tears and said, "I'm proud of you."

Jude remembered feeling her hand slip out of his as he backed away. She and Sarah gripped each other for strength, leaning on each other in permanent station. Widowed in the same month, and now saying goodbye to their sons on the same day, they knew a kinship most never would.

Jude was glad they had each other. He was glad Mae wouldn't be alone. He was glad to know Sarah would still walk over for breakfast every morning, and that knowledge was the only thing that got his first leg over the side of the skiff.

In between the paddles that pushed him toward the Refuge, Jude garnered enough courage to glance back. He tried to make out Mae's expression—tried to grasp any indication that she was okay. But the glisten of the sun reflecting off her face blinded him to any detail there.

Nothing more than tears and the sun's reflection. Those were the only two things that kept him blind enough to keep him moving that day.

PRESENT DAY

Jude wondered why the thought of returning to Zoar caused his stomach to churn as much as it did. Whether simply caused by the urgency of getting Collette to safety; or the tear of competing purposes; or was it the lingering guilt he felt at abandoning the women who'd raised him? There was no doubt that the direction he sailed stirred a deep unsettling in him.

He exhaled deeply against Collette's arms still wrapped around him—his greatest comfort and greatest fear existing in one embrace.

He had six months to get her home and a journey that should only take three. The dangers that existed on the seas of Physis were innumerable—especially for a crew that didn't fly allegiance to any one territory. Especially for a crew full of mutants. Especially for a captain and wife who didn't match.

And most especially for a child who would be born of the both of them.

Zoar was the only safe place for them to exist, and Jude had to get them home.

CHAPTER FOUR

MAE

PRESENT DAY

Zoar

Mae sat beside Sarah and watched her sleep. It'd been a week since she'd stumbled through the door and onto the kitchen floor. After regaining consciousness, Mae had helped her friend to the daybed in which she remained.

Some days brought small improvements in Sarah's condition, but the fever that had swept the island was unforgiving. Mae tried not to listen to the stories, but they consumed as hungrily as the fever did.

Sarah stirred and cleared her throat of its unuse. "Are the boys back?" she whispered.

Mae sighed and rubbed her friend's hand gently. Over the last few days, Sarah had asked the question several times. Always the same question. Always the same answer.

"No, darling," Mae said. "Not yet."

Sarah turned in the daybed while sleep overcame her again. Mae rested her head back into the soft chair she'd pulled nearby. She looked around the open room that composed her kitchen and living spaces. Open, wide, and white, the buildings on the island did everything they could to keep the temperature in their homes at a tolerable level. The space was unremarkable apart from the crafted driftwood furniture that decorated it. The carpenter was a true craftsman and his work a trademark of the island.

Mae loved that furniture. To her, it was a physical symbol of the best parts of Zoar. What others considered discardable, the carpenter made into beautiful, unique, one-of-a-kind pieces that sung originality and beauty in ways that conformity could not.

She let her eyes fall on her favorite piece in the room—the dining table. The oblong shape was far from nameable, and it wove in unpredictable grooves and swerves. Its knots were spontaneous and its top uneven and it stood on a base of teak that grew four legs out from its center. Its collective pieces would have been trash anywhere else, but in Zoar, it was made into a stunning, functional table that had long ago become the nexus of her home.

As she considered it, that table was the central place of the most meaningful, most memorable events that occurred in her life. It was sitting at that table, looking her family members in the eyes, that every big conversation took place. It's where honesty happened. It's where pain was processed and where joys were shared. It's where lessons were taught and where patience was learned. It's where Sarah had stumbled in just a few days earlier.

And it's where the four of them sat the morning the boys decided to leave.

TWO YEARS EARLIER

"Morning, Mama."

Jonathan pecked Mae on the cheek and dipped a hand into the pan in front of her.

"Get out of her cooking, boy!" Sarah scolded behind him. She swatted at the air and shooed him away from the stove.

"Where's Jude?" Jonathan asked.

Mae tipped her head in the direction of Jude's bedroom and watched Jonathan disappear.

"You're worried."

Sarah stated her observation of Mae plainly.

"He needs purpose," Mae shook her head, helpless. "I can't give him that."

"No one can," answered Sarah.

Mae nodded her agreement. "I'm just afraid of what he'll choose if he can't find it. We watch these boys do it all the time."

Sarah shook her head in response. "He's not gonna fight," she said matter-of-factly.

Mae pulled one side of her mouth back in thought. "Put Jonathan on it," she suggested. "Maybe he can talk him into being a healer, too." Mae chuckled and waved her spoon down the hall. "Then they can hang out all the time."

Sarah laughed, "You know I can't talk any more sense into mine than you can into yours."

Sarah sat back in her chair and crossed one leg over the other. "If I could, do you really think he'd have tattoos over every inch of his body?" She pursed her lips. "And, Lord, I would've made him cut his hair and shave his face years ago."

Laughter filled the kitchen like the song under a waterfall, and Mae was thankful for the relief of it.

"Who's sharing the joke?" Jonathan asked, as he and Jude joined them.

Mae and Sarah stifled their laughter while Mae carried breakfast to the table.

"Let's eat," Mae redirected, still ridding herself of muffled chuckles.

She seated herself and took one of the boys' hands in each of hers. For twenty years they'd eaten breakfast like this—here; together. So many meals, they could not be numbered. So many conversations, they could not be bottled. So much value, it would never be measured.

Mae looked at the hands that made up her family—each one so different from the next. Each shade and shape so starkly contrasted from the one it held. Zoar was the only place in Physis this could occur. It was why she'd come. It was why she'd stayed.

She breathed satisfaction at the sight of her friend and their two grown sons circled around another meal together.

"We wanted to talk to you about something," Jude announced, hesitantly.

"Grace first," Sarah said.

Unease grew in Mae's stomach and threw knots at her. She'd known mornings like this one were numbered, but she didn't expect a decision quite so soon. She didn't know what Jude was about to say, but she knew it would be her job to support it—support him—when it happened.

And now the moment had arrived, a thief come to join them at their shared table.

She locked eyes with Sarah from across the table. Her friend was reading her mind and she knew it. Sarah offered her a nod of assurance that said all it needed to, and she offered thanks over their meal without being asked.

Only a soul friend could read a mind like that. And only Sarah could do it for Mae.

They took a collective breath and braced for impact.

PRESENT DAY

Mae reflected on what it felt like to have Jude announce his plan that morning. And she remembered the look on Sarah's face when Jonathan said he'd be leaving, too.

She looked from the charactered table where it had all taken place, to her sickly sleeping friend beside her. Her labored breaths tattered up and down in unsettled spurts.

They'd lived a lot of life together and each had taken her turns leaning on the other. But the morning the boys declared their plans, they both knew the next part of their journey was going to push them in hard, unbending, and unforgiving ways.

Even so, Mae never expected this. She patted perspiration off Sarah's forehead and repositioned the pillow under her head. She wished Sarah could receive a reassuring gesture from her like she'd offered that morning. She wished she could tell her the boys had returned when next she asked. And she wished her friend would recover, if only so that she wouldn't have to wait alone anymore.

Mae laid a hand on Sarah's shoulder and left her to step out onto the porch that overlooked the eastern sea and skyline. She could see Sarah's empty house down the hill and felt its emptiness match her own.

With her friend asleep inside and the day nearing its end, there was nothing left to do but stare at the horizon and will the masts of the Refuge to break its weary line.

CHAPTER FIVE

MATTHEW

The Diamond Isles

Matthew followed his father onto the boat that would carry them the short distance to Triton. His feet weighed heavier than they ever had. He'd made weak attempts to mask the blend of fear and resentment that wrecked his insides but knew he wasn't getting the job done. In truth, he didn't care to.

The sound of the angry waves that had been his perpetual serenade helped steady him again last night. He related to them, being thrust upon unmoving walls of diamonds, and being pulled back only to be thrust upon them again. They were mad. And they were helpless against the will of the sea. Just as he was.

And it was that same immoveable will of the sea that forced him against his instincts now, too. Triton would be within sight in the next twenty minutes, and on it would be living proof of the damage the Diamond Isles royalty had done—damage of what generations of his family had preserved.

The sole leader in trade imports and exports, the Diamond Isles had been the financial superpower in Physis for decades. It'd started in the mining of its namesake—diamonds. After mining enough from the Diamond Isles, Matthew's great, great, great grandfather had purchased Triton. Triton was a massive piece of land stocked full of not only diamonds, but several other mineable resources not limited to copper, silver, nickel, cobalt, and chromium. After the acquisition of the land, the isles needed a workforce able to mine the invaluable worth Triton offered. So, Matthew's great, great, great-grandfather had done what he knew he could do. He exiled the tainted, or what the isles dubbed recessives, with their mixed blood lines and unsightly deformations, and created a workforce. They were paid enough to eat, but hardly more than that. By limiting their compensation and their ability to thrive independently, the isles could keep the workforce close, essentially disallowing them to leave by limiting their means to do so. All the profits of their labor would be allocated directly to the isles and would be used for the purchase of additional land and loyalties—or filtered right into the isle's war efforts. A massive export business along with handsome loans to poorer territories to keep them in the war positioned the isles in a sustained state of authority in Physis. It was a position that won them several allies—and several enemies— most of whom lived close by, on Triton.

Unrest among Triton recessives had been simmering under the surface for a long while. But with a new and power-hungry foreman in the mines, it was getting worse by the day. Not helping the matter was the reality that most of the workforce had lost family to the war. Whether they were currently out fighting or had already been lost, nearly every recessive working a Triton mine had sacrificed at least one loved one to the Diamond Isles cause—a cause not their own.

The unrest had recently become enough of a challenge that

the foreman had requested the presence of the king.

Matthew wondered if it would help. The king seemed to think it would.

Matthew speculated as to whether Triton inhabitants would know him or recognize who he was. It was the first time they would see their to-be-king. Matthew hoped curiosity would outrank whatever resentment they were sure to have toward him.

"Ah. There we are." The king nodded at the land pushing through the fog on the horizon. "Triton."

Matthew looked up from the dark sea to the bank of the massive land before him. Its mountains dwarfed those of the Diamond Isles, bigger and grander than anything Matthew had ever seen in person. He shook at the noticeable drop in temperature and let goosebumps run their way up and down his body. The cold sunk into him swimming alongside the fear that grew like the mountainous peaks before him.

The sky was darker here. The clouds lower. The wind stronger, more cutting than anything he'd felt. The footman aboard draped cloaks on both he and his father and disappeared below deck without comment. A habit well-rehearsed, it seemed.

"The land is so grand. It's as if it brings the sea to its end." Matthew couldn't disguise the surprise in his voice. Having never departed from the isles, his expectations shrank before him like a leaf in a flame.

The king laughed. "No, the sea goes well beyond Triton's borders and more, but I see how you could think it."

Matthew drank in the newness before him. "I've never seen so many buildings. They're dull—like many small boxes. Why are they so close together? Why not a more generous use of the land? There's space on the mountains. And why is it so cold here?"

Questions flew through his mind faster than he could make sense of them.

"Well, most of Triton is not fit for living. You see where that mountain range begins?" The king pointed. "The tainted mine all of those we can reach, but the conditions are far too harsh past that for habitation. The winds are high, and snow and ice come year-round. Here next to the sea, the residents are sheltered from the harshest weather, and they can exist here, closest to the mines they work."

Matthew's expression changed. "That's funny," he replied.

"What's that?" asked the king.

"You said 'we' ...all those mountains *we* can reach... like you mine them yourself."

Matthew snorted derisively while his eyes glazed into molasses. Matthew watched his father wordlessly deflate from the moment and turn to watch their final approach to Triton. Matthew wanted to care that he had ruined the moment between them; but he didn't.

"Matthew. Come."

The king tipped his chin at Matthew, directing him over to where he stood, ready to depart the vessel. As Matthew submitted, royal guardians surrounded him and his father in a box and lifted body-length shields on each side. Matthew couldn't see beyond them. The guards readied weapons behind their shields and walked in unison to his and the king's strides, bringing the protective cave alongside their bodies every step of the way.

Matthew was only seconds away from complaining that he could not see beyond the wall when he heard the first PING!

"What was that?!" he shouted.

Then another. PING! And a third. PING!

Matthew could not comprehend it.

The residents of Triton were throwing food at the marching royal guard. Food and rocks hit the shields the officers carried and fell to the ground at Matthew's feet. Beyond the cocoon, he could hear the shouting: "Diamond scum!" "Go back to your castle!" "Don't catch a cold!" "How dare you come here!" "Keep the guard close, king!"

"Blasphemy!" Matthew thought.

No matter the discord Matthew had with his father he couldn't stand for Diamond Isles royalty to be treated with such open disdain.

"Father, do something! How can you let them speak to us like this?" Matthew protested.

"Just walk, Matthew."

The king replied calmly, seemingly unmoved by the spectacle.

Matthew's mind went blank as they walked. He focused on his father's steps in front of him and didn't look up until they stopped moving. They were inside somewhere dark, and the silence Matthew usually disdained finally reclaimed space enough for him to welcome it. The royal guard dispersed to a large, dark meeting room where the foreman stood with several of his high-ranking employees. Its cave-like walls looked as if they'd been formed of dirt or clay, and the floor they stood upon was nothing more than grassless earth. Matthew had never seen anything so dank. The royal family's horses lived higher than this.

"King, you didn't tell me you were bringing your son, we are so honor—"

The king cut him off, "Cleopas, why have the people not been restrained? We have discussed this too many times. If you cannot get Triton under control, I will have no choice but to find a leader who can. I thought that's why I chose you in the first place."

"Forgive me, King, it is not so bad as it seems. We've just had a few harsh weather days. You know what that can do to people. We'll get a warm, dry day and they'll see reason again. Surely, they will."

Matthew did not miss the eye roll from the man standing behind Cleopas. The small noise that escaped him along with it was enough to get him a shooting glare from Cleopas that demanded his silence on the matter.

Cleopas turned all his sniveling attention to Matthew. "Prince Matthew, what an honor to have you here. We have desired to host you here on Triton for ages. May I have the honor of touring you around the facilities?"

There was no choice in the matter. It was the reason the king had insisted Matthew come. It was time for him to learn the business.

Inside the plants and mines, the sentiment toward the royal family was only slightly warmer. There was none so brave as to shout profanities at the king or Matthew in such close proximities, but Matthew could sense the tension that filled the air they pushed through.

Matthew traveled a few steps behind the king and Cleopas, trying to focus on Cleopas' tour but too distracted to hear it. He couldn't pull his attention from the watching recessives—men and women, young and old. He watched them and they watched him. Most of their dirtied faces turned first to the king with malice and then softened when they realized he had company.

Matthew imagined what it may have been like to hear about a prince for decades, but never see one. Something like that would most certainly spark any number of rumors among the people of Triton.

But they wouldn't wonder now. For now, they seemed far too curious to be angry—at least for the moment.

Matthew and the Triton recessives' reflective curiosities were enough to carry him through to the end of the tour and they were reboarding the royal vessel before he knew it. He hadn't captured any of his intended education, but he knew he would never forget the dark sets of eyes that had stared back at him.

The journey home was quiet.

Matthew watched the ship push back from Triton and noted that somewhere in the day he'd begun to ignore the knots in his stomach. They were still there; but he'd been too taken by his own fascination to pay any more attention to them. He'd known there was hostility for the Diamond Isles, the royal family, and the rest of the pures, but he had no idea it was so dense—so palpable.

His father, who held himself so regally, so proudly, had walked through hordes of people shouting profanities at him and throwing food at him like it was nothing. He took it like it was just another day. Matthew wondered why his father continued to visit Triton knowing that's what awaited him. He wondered why the king had never mentioned it. Was it simply out of pride? Matthew wondered if his mother knew. He wondered why his father hadn't prepared him for it. And more importantly, he wondered why the king hadn't yet put an end to it. He was the king, after all.

Matthew had entered the day dreading what he would face, and he left it more familiar with discomfort than he'd ever wished to be. How could he possibly take over as king of the Diamond Isles and Triton? He had no idea how to deal with these kinds of politics. He'd never wanted the job before. He was sure he didn't want it now.

He wanted to jump off the side of the ship and swim until he couldn't anymore. And he would have seriously considered it if not for his mother. He would give almost anything to escape the future that had been assigned him.

The king approached him from below deck, his expression as it always was, as if nothing new had happened.

"Matthew, several meets with potential matches have been scheduled for you for tomorrow. You'll choose one to marry by the end of the week, or I'll choose for you. We won't discuss it again."

And with that, the king was gone, leaving only the icy air of the isles behind him.

CHAPTER SIX

ISSACHAR

Agon

Issachar paced the floor of the main barracks. He considered that though this was his fifth time around, it didn't feel any easier than the previous.

His heart raced wildly, and he didn't waste any effort at trying to contain it. He let nervous energy consume his body entirely and order him any way it desired.

It was his way. It always had been.

Against all the battle training he'd ever received, Issachar knew that for him, the best way to fight was to let the energy take over—wild or tamed. To Issachar this was the way of the true warrior. The genuine warrior was the one who was willing to feel the fear wholly—every terrifying and trembling ounce of it—and let it own him all the way down through his bones.

Whether rage, or fear, or anxiety, or thrill, or pride—he did well to let the emotion fuel him, to take him over and consume him completely. Emotions knew his soul better than he did, and they ordered his movements with an instinct he could not, and did not, want to tame.

As a young warrior Issachar learned that all nature and no discipline was a distinct foolishness. He'd seen too many soldiers fall because they couldn't find a balance between the two. So there was a limit to how long he let emotion run unhindered in him. He was more effective in battle when he allowed his nature to order his strikes, but there was a ledge to the instinctual beast, and he had to learn when to pull back and force his mind to lead his machine again. It was a delicate balance, and Issachar preferred the spirit to the mind. Knowing how to manage the two together is what separated him from the herd on the battlefield.

At nineteen years old, the youngest in Agonian history, Issachar battled his way into chieftain rank. The way of Agon was war. No leader achieved chieftain rank through anything but his kill count. On the war front and the training field, Issachar was a force unmatched. His leaders and peers knew from his earliest years that he would lead Agon. Everyone knew. Even other territories knew. News from the warfront travelled to every corner of Physis of Issachar—a name to be feared; a warrior; a conqueror.

The muscles stacked in his arms folded onto each other, twitching with anticipation as they did before a battle. He pushed his knuckles into dark skin and evened his breaths by an internal count. The door before him opened heavily while Issachar's searching eyes consumed the sight in front of him.

Relief and wonder flooded him.

"Father," Eden said, greeting him. "May I introduce you to your fifth daughter, Elysian."

Issachar watched his eldest daughter smile into the face of the wrapped babe in her arms as she lifted her up to meet him. Issachar's massive and warworn forearms took the tiny bundle with a practiced tenderness.

He knew this skill just as intimately as he knew battle. It

was one of the two things he treasured most in life. Warrior and chieftain, he was, but father and adorer he was primarily. They were the titles that fueled his choices. They drove purpose into the fierce protection their land and community required.

And now, all *six* of his girls, including his beloved wife, were here to protect as well.

Issachar freely let tears roll down his marked face while greeting his newest child. He smiled at Eden and asked, "your mother?"

"She's well," she answered easily.

Issachar could not believe how Eden had grown into such a beautiful young woman. He remembered vividly the day he'd received Eden this way, on her first day in the world.

He nodded contentedly at the news of his wife's wellbeing and carefully turned to face the firelit corridor that would begin the child's introduction to her new world. Torches threw dancing shadows across the dirt floor, and he stepped forward onto them slowly. Issachar knew they were waiting, but he wasn't going to rush it.

This was tradition. It was too important to hurry.

He began with the drawings closest to him. He turned the baby to face the color that covered the stone walls that surrounded them.

"Little firefly, *this is Agon.*"

With those familiar words, the chief began to tell his newest daughter the history of the land he loved and lived to protect.

He pointed to each drawing along the wall, recounting the histories with the greatest detail.

"You see, Agon is the largest territory in Physis. You see how big it is compared to the others? We have things here that help take care of you, and your sisters, and your mother, and all the special people who live here." He continued, "we have fresh water, and lots of land we can use to grow food, and lots of people who do jobs that keep us living well."

Issachar moved to a new set of paintings on the wall.

"But, my love, when you have a gift like this land and the special people of Agon, someone is always going to want to take it from you. That is our burden. And your father," he pointed to himself, "that's me. I'm in charge of making sure we protect that special gift.

"Now Agon is special because we have very big and strong fighting men who dedicate their lives to protecting us and our land. Papa is one of those, too." He smiled at her, "yes, I am. I'm the leader of them. We start our boys early, and we teach them how to be strong warriors so beautiful little girls like you and your sisters and your mother stay safe."

Issachar moved to the last group of paintings.

"And you know what? It works. You see here," Issachar pointed to the drawings on the walls. "These are the many, many ships and men we have. And these are the many, many battles we have won. We have more fighting men than everyone else, and we win more battles than all the rest of Physis. That's how we stay safe."

Issachar reached the last drawing on the wall. It was a bow and arrow crossed by a sword, pointing in opposite directions.

"And this, little firefly, is the most important part of Agon. It means, 'Agon for Agon.' We do not mix with other territories. We keep to Agon. Your friends will be Agonian; your parents are Agonian; your sisters are Agonian. The way we stay safe is to keep together."

Issachar exhaled a deep smile onto the infant he held. He kissed her lightly on the forehead, as he had his previous four daughters before this moment.

"Are you ready?" he whispered over her.

He paused for one final moment, and then pushed open the large steel door that opened out into the jungle night air. Outside the chief's barracks, a mass of people—his people— waited quietly in the black. They stood silently, anticipating the newest chieftain family member, each holding candles that lit up their dark and beautiful faces.

Perhaps his favorite of all Agon's grand traditions, the chief would walk through the sea of people, the people he lived to protect, and each would reach in to touch him as he held his new child. He locked eyes with the men he fought next to, their strong hands squeezing his shoulder as he walked by. He smiled onto children who cautiously approached to lift small hands to timidly brush one of his massive thighs. Elderly men and women came knowingly, nodding their approval and resting gentle warmth on his forearms, blessing him and the child.

The walk would take hours, but each Agonian would know that little Elysian had been welcomed properly into her people, having been told the history from whence she came, the loyalty to which she now belonged, and the importance of what she too, would now live to protect.

CHAPTER SEVEN

JUDE

The Physis Sea

Thunder from the guns in the belly of the approaching ship sounded too loudly for Jude to hear his fellow crewmate's straining words. The sea water splashed up from the explosions like backward rain and Jude squinted to try to see through it. He screamed over the sound but only produced soundlessness against the tumult. He worked his eyes back and forth through the chaos to find the Refuge through the wall of water behind him, but it was gone. Had they left him? His crewmate continued to yell inaudible messages at him, but nothing could pull him into focus.

Just then, a new blast smashed into the bow of their skiff and darkness enveloped him as the dark water became his new nightfall. He sank deeper and deeper until his lungs and ears burned under the pressure. Jude tried to find the surface but struggled to make out the grey of the sky from the break of the surface of the sea. He worked his arms against the water, becoming more desperate for a breath with every extended second.

Where was the surface? Where was the oxygen that his lungs screamed to attain? Where was the Refuge?

And where, he was afraid to wonder, was Collette?

Jude shot up from his bed, inhaling oxygen in gulps of relief. He was drenched in sweat and breathing heavily from the seeming realness of his nightmare. Collette stirred and reached for him, still half asleep.

"Jude? Are you okay?" she asked.

"Yeah," he forced big, full breaths of air into his chest.

"Yes," he said again. He lifted her hand to his mouth and kissed it, "I'm fine. Go back to sleep."

Collette sleepily agreed. The pregnancy had made her so tired he wasn't going to steal a minute of her sleep that he didn't have to.

He dressed and headed above deck to breathe in the sea air. Not a lot could calm him like it could. He wanted to hear the rhythm of the water against the belly of the ship. He wanted to hear the ropes croak against the wind. He wanted salt on his skin and the familiar cry of seagulls dressing the sky.

As he broke to the deck he inhaled again, deeply, and sighed relief into the expansive sky above him. He walked to the bow and leaned against the rail of the Refuge, endless navy blue in front and below him. It was terrifying, and it was wonderful, and it was the very reason he loved it. One could not be fooled into believing he could control the sea. It had to be respected and it had to be feared. There was nothing Jude or anyone else could do to tame the beast that was the ocean. She was in control, and she was all around. She was the great equalizer. In the acceptance of that, Jude found freedom.

"Brother."

Jude turned at the sound of Jonathan's voice coming from behind him. There he stood, at the helm, consistent as ever.

"Couldn't sleep?" Jonathan asked him.

"No," Jude replied. "You either?"

Jonathan lifted one side of his mouth and shook his head.

They stood in silence for a while, not requiring the other to fill the air. After a while, Jude spoke. "Do you remember the first time we were boarded?"

Jonathan groaned and nodded his affirmation of the unpleasant memory.

"It haunts me, Jonathan. I keep seeing the ship come up on us fast like it did, and I keep seeing the ropes coming over the quarter deck and the crew coming in. And I keep seeing them bring Collette up from below, you know? The look she had on her face—begging me to do something—to save her. I've never felt so helpless."

Jude paused while the memory swept him.

"She's my wife, Jonathan. She's my wife and I couldn't do anything to help her."

Jude's voice started to break with emotion.

"She's okay, Jude. She wasn't taken. And just now she sleeps soundly below, happy as ever, and growing your child."

The reminder of the urgency of his task met Jude again with Jonathan's words.

"We have to get her home. What was I thinking bringing her on this mission with us? I never should have let her come."

Jonathan laughed at his friend.

"How could you have prevented it? There's no way she would've let you come without her. She would've hidden in the linens or disguised herself as a man. She would have lived covered in chicken crap and hid in the coop below before she would've let you do this without her."

It was enough to force a grin to Jude's face.

"You're right about that," he chuckled, picturing his beloved decorated in chicken feathers.

Jude watched his friend laugh and nod his agreement, his eyes never leaving the horizon. Jonathan had been there from the beginning and worked side-by-side with Collette since the conception of the Refuge mission. He knew her well. Almost as well as Jude did. And Jude knew his friend was right.

Collette was just as much invested in the Refuge mission as anyone else. She'd been there at the beginning. She'd encouraged it. She'd nailed new boards into its side right alongside Jude. She'd sweat into its wooden deck and sanded and painted its panels alongside the crew. She'd scouted and stacked supplies through all hours of the night in the days leading up to their departure. In many ways, she was the mission.

Jude sank back into his present reality.

"I think about that day, and the many times we've been boarded since then, and I can't help but wonder what would happen if someone did take her. And now I don't risk losing only her, but my child as well."

Jude shook his head at the thought, hoping it would shake out of his consciousness.

"And you know what they would do to a blended child," he added.

The statement lingered in the air like a stench.

"I can't lose them, Jonathan."

Jonathan didn't answer, but Jude felt his friend grip his shoulder from behind him. There weren't words enough, so they stood in silence until the moon rose high enough to sparkle life onto the sea around them, and then begin its slow descent.

CHAPTER EIGHT

JONATHAN

At the helm, Jonathan gripped the wood of the wheel and squeezed the muscles in his jaw until his teeth hurt. He felt Jude's fear viscerally, like it was part of his own body. The idea of Collette being taken had haunted him too, since the very first time it happened...

A YEAR AND A HALF EARLIER

Jonathan was below deck with Collette, the infirmary beds nearly full that day. They'd spent a spell closer to the action over the last few weeks and floated away when their capacity filled to its maximum with the injured. It'd taken a fortnight or so, but people started to heal and left the ward floor of the Refuge for their respective territories or fleets.

Several territories were represented on the ship at any

given time, and it had a tendency to lead to conflict in every corner of the Refuge vessel. Life was a constant battle—onboard and off. They'd just returned from a nearby territory to dispense of some of the healed when it happened. The crew had been so anxious to rid itself of the onboard tension they'd missed the pursuit of the coming ship.

Jonathan and Collette were folding clean linens and laughing at the eccentricities of a patient who couldn't help but confess all his dark, childhood secrets in his sleepy, medicinal trance. Whether a side effect of the war trauma or his medication, the patient eagerly spilled the secrets of his past to the surrounding crew and patients. He weepily confessed of stealing candy from local traders, and regrettably recalled trespassing on neighbors' properties to spy on young ladies. Earlier in the day he'd defended his choice to plant frogs in his sister's bed because she wouldn't let him play with her toy train—although, for that also, he was very sorry.

His stories and regrets were endless to the point that Davies, the patient next to sleep talker, called out to Jonathan and Collette for mercy. "Docs, you gotta move me to one of those back bunks. I can't sleep with this guy's Hail Marys in my ear. I can't take any more of this."

Jonathan and Collette laughed together before Jonathan dropped his folded linens in the pile.

"Of course," he said. "Come on, I'll help you get back there."

Jonathan hoisted Davies up and helped him hobble to a quieter corner of the ward floor.

Jonathan was only just returning to the medical table when unrecognizable men came bursting through the doors.

Jonathan remembered the strangers' unsettling pleasure at finding a woman aboard—let alone one as pleasing to the eye as Collette. And against all of Jonathan's efforts and proffers to trade his life for hers, they took her handedly, and not without giving Jonathan a swift and forceful beating that was enough to knock him unconscious.

Jonathan assumed they marched her out the door and above deck, because by the time he was conscious again, she was nowhere to be found in the ward. He was bound by the men who stayed back, and he wrestled them up to open air while the rest of the alien crew ransacked what resources they could on the Refuge.

Above deck, Jonathan was forced to his knees while he tried to hold his eyes open against their instantaneous swelling. He saw Jude's face. It was a look on his brother's face he would not forget. It was sheer desperation—like Jonathan had never seen before—not even on a patient who knew the surety of his own death.

He didn't have to wonder. He knew. Losing Collette would be worse than dying to Jude.

It would be worse for Jonathan as well.

Jonathan stayed trained on Jude's stare, which clung to the visual of his wife being held by the animals of men who had taken her. Jonathan could see Jude trying to calm himself in the moment, not wanting to give away who Collette was to him—trying to evade the value of what the men held in their hungry hands.

The foreign captain approached Jude.

"Captain, if I'm not mistaken? Your crew looks to you."

It was true. The ragtag crew of mutants that made up the Refuge all turned their hope to Jude. Their fearful and inquisitive eyes searched him for cues on how to respond; for answers on what to do next; for calm in the chaos.

They'd all known this was a possibility, but it was a first— for nearly all of them.

The man didn't wait for a response.

"Well then, Captain. Where are your colors? Your absence of allegiance leads me to believe you are the enemy of Physis." The man yelled the last part, "which makes you an enemy to me."

Jude shook his head. "We are no one's enemy. We fly no colors because we do not fight."

At this, the man blasted Jude in the gut with an unforgiving kick.

"Do you still not fight?" he asked, snarling.

"We heal the injured and return them to their homes," Jude winced against the pain. "That is all."

"That's all?" The man snorted his response in derision. "You defeat our purposes by returning men to a fight we've already taken them out of. By that alone, you do not only fight against my people, but you curse your own by not picking up arms for them."

Then, the man turned and spoke to the whole crew. "You *are* my enemy," he nodded. "And, by the sound of it, you are an enemy to all of Physis!"

Jonathan watched while in a pregnant moment, the foreign captain seemed to notice the thing he'd been missing since he'd arrived on the ship. The thing that single-handedly put the crew of the Refuge at its greatest risk. The man's gaze lifted and dropped as it connected one Refuge crewman to the other in a smooth and flowing motion. He spun around slowly as he collected visible information on each of them—not one the same. Some mutants. Some mixed. Some limbless.

"What is this?" He yielded and readied his weapon as he asked, as did each of the men with him in succession. "You are among the tainted! You have blood from twenty different territories onboard this vessel!" The man pointed at Chef Jackson, "You have mutants onboard!" His voice raised in pitch and volume, laying bare his anger and fear like a curtain pulled too early.

Jonathan watched Jude gather himself. This is what they knew would happen. They'd discussed it many times. Jude was prepared for this fight—just not the one in which Collette was being contained. Jonathan knew Jude could handle this part. He watched him breathe and waited for him to speak the words they'd practiced.

"We are all different, yes, but we are all human. Many places, but one people. We offer no harm to you or anyone else. We just want to help."

A foreign crew member gasped behind Jonathan and shouted out, "it's the Heap, captain! They come from the Heap!" The man in front of Jude snapped to him for confirmation.

Jude nodded. "Yes, we come from Zoar."

The foreign captain lowered his weapon, his tone changing from anger to mockery.

"Well, well," he smirked, "I always wondered what it looked like on the Heap. Now I don't have to waste the months getting there to find out." He eyed the Zoarian crew, judging each with disapproval and spit at their feet. "Trash," he sniveled, "adequately named."

The man's crew laughed at his remark, ridiculing the disheveled group at their mercy.

Jonathan hoped these last insults would mean it was over, but when the foreign captain departed from Jude, he approached Chef Jackson, who was bound along with the rest of the crew. The man's countenance shot from arrogance to anger in the flash of a moment, as fear of the mutated overcame him.

He screamed at Jude from across the deck. "The Heap mocks Physis by keeping mutants alive! How dare you use them to aid in saving another?!"

In a swift motion he raised his sword readying to strike Chef Jackson, but not before Collette shrieked her objection. She strained against her handlers and yelled. "No!"

The man froze at the sound of a woman's voice and lead dropped into the pit of Jonathan's stomach. The one place he'd wished the man would not find focus for his eyes was now the center of his every affection.

The man looked Collette up and down and slowly let out a

grotesque, "my, my."

Jonathan glanced at Jude to confirm the agony he felt. Of course, it was there too. Jonathan prayed Jude would keep his composure.

The foreign captain continued, "perhaps it's not all trash you keep in the Heap."

He greedily lifted Collette's chin to him, just inches from his face, and Jonathan knew it would mean the end of Jude's restraint. In one blink, Jude, who had remained the epitome of calm throughout the commandeering, now uncontrollably thrashed against his captors in thoughtless reaction. Jonathan cringed, knowing the weight of what Jude had just given away. It was exactly what they had agreed could not be revealed if ever this happened.

The foreign leader showed instant recognition to Jude's response.

"She's yours," he said plainly. "You can see why I wouldn't have guessed it," he said pointing back and forth between the two of them. He smirked. "You know, in every territory except for yours, this is punishable by death." He lifted his shoulders mockingly, "but I'm sure you know that, don't you?"

Jonathan watched the man leave Collette to return to his attention to Jude. He couldn't help but feel relieved in the man's repositioning. The man continued, "I must give it to you though, captain, although she's clearly recessive, she's quite the beauty." He smiled as the devil, himself. "Can't say I blame you."

After a heavy pause, he concluded. "Very well," he said dramatically, "we will leave you be." Then he turned to face Collette and said to the men holding her, "she comes with us."

Panic washed over Jonathan as the statement sunk in. In unthinking reaction, he screamed. "No! Please! No! She's my wife! She's my wife!"

The foreign captain paused. He looked freshly at Jonathan, not needing a previous reason to bother with him, and then back to Collette. "*Your* wife?"

Jonathan nodded furiously, making no effort to hide his panic.

The man angled his head to the side, displaying his confoundment at the statement. "Then why the emotion from your captain?"

"She is our healer," Jonathan answered quickly. "The captain would not want to lose our greatest asset. As you know, healing is the reason we're out here." Jonathan paused, his eyes pleading for him. "He did not want to give away her value. None of us did."

A foreign crewman piped in, "'Tis right, cap'n. They was down below the two of 'em together. Down in the healing rooms with the sick 'ens—'tis where we found 'em."

Jonathan could see the foreign captain consider this, hoping he didn't feel quite as free to take a rightly matched man from his wife—even if it was a lie. Physis law would support taking Collette from Jude, the two obviously birthed of different territories. But Physis law would not support separating Collette from Jonathan, who were obviously matched recessives.

While Jonathan watched the foreign captain consider this, a man limped out from below deck, two of the invading crewmen supporting him from either side.

"Cap'n! We found Davies below!"

The men struggled to hold up the patient. It was the man who had asked Jonathan for reprieve from the sleep talker just before the ordeal began. He was the one Jonathan helped hobble to the quiet corner of the ward floor.

The foreign captain turned on Jude and shouted in anger. "You hold captive one of my men?!"

Jude shook his head, "no." He sighed audible relief and softened his voice. "Captain, we *healed* one of your men."

In the foreign captain's astonished silence, Jude added, "he's free to go, as they all are."

The man stood flummoxed. Jonathan watched as his anger turned to astonishment, and now turned to what could only be described as shame. Davies must have meant something to the foreign captain and his crew. If they had no other understanding of humanity, they at least understood loyalty. It had to have informed their code in some way, because their obviously shifted countenance both covered them, and undisguised them all at once.

It was quick after that.

With the resolve of a leader well-tuned to decision-making, the foreign captain replaced his sword into its sheath and ordered his crew's departure from the Refuge. They were the two most relieving words Jonathan had ever heard.

"Let's go."

Jonathan acted swiftly.

"Darling," he called to Collette.

He waved her over to him. Collette played along, running to him, and wrapping her arms around him like he'd watched her do to Jude a thousand times before. He could feel her heart pounding against him and felt her head raise slightly to shoot a quick and inconspicuous look to Jude, who stood across the deck trained on her every move.

What was every bit a show to Collette, felt much less-so to Jonathan. He knew it was wrong. He knew he would never, could never, act on it. And he knew that this moment would only last for a flicker.

So, for that one moment, as escaping as it was, he imprinted into his memory what it felt like to have her arms solidly latched around him.

While the moon hung high in its place above them, Jonathan wondered if Jude was reliving the ordeal like he was. He wondered how Jude remembered it, and if it haunted him in just the same ways.

Jude turned and placed a strong hand on his brother's shoulder. "I'm going to go check on her."

Jonathan lifted one side his mouth and dipped his chin.

He was glad for it—even if it wasn't him who had the honor of doing the checking.

CHAPTER NINE

MATTHEW

The Diamond Isles

Matthew sat at the tea table across from a beautiful woman, who wore a lace-trimmed gown that must have taken hours to put on and years to make. She seemed severely uncomfortable, and she moved in short, tense arrangements as if she was afraid a just-wrong turn would cause her to shatter to a thousand pieces. To Matthew, she appeared like an all-too-small teacup that can only exist as a decoration on a shelf— beautiful, but far too delicate to be functional.

As uncomfortable and dull as she was, he preferred her to the one with whom he'd dined at breakfast. The early visitor was energetic and chatty and reeked of a desperation too great to be filled by any one human—and it certainly wasn't going to be him.

This set of endless visits with potential matches was the summation of his days since he'd returned from Triton. He would have been wearied of it by now even if he'd wanted to do it in the first place.

The fact was, though, that he didn't want to do it. He didn't want any of it. He didn't want to be king. He questioned every principle the isles stood upon. He had no desire to bear the weight of his father's crown, and surely had no interest in a hand-selected wife, qualifiable only by her blood line, genetics, and family's mining investments.

After dutifully escorting the mousey teacup of a woman to the front door and bidding her adieu, Matthew sulked to his mother's bedside. She was spending more and more time there, to Matthew's great dread.

"Darling," she smiled at him. "Come. Tell me all about the girls today." She waved him over to her bedside and took his hand.

"Mother," he sighed and pressed his forehead to the hand holding his, "I don't want this."

"Don't worry, my love, the right one will come. You'll see."

Matthew lifted his head to meet her lovely pale face and wondered how much to share with her. He feared disappointing her in what would surely be her last months of living. He wondered if his silence about the doubts he felt was a more merciful choice for his beloved mother, than the truth that he questioned the foundations from which he came.

Through blurry eyes he broke.

"No, mother," he cracked under emotion. "That's not it. I don't want to be king. I'm not made for it. I hate the politics. I hate faking what I believe."

He looked at her with a passion far short of what he felt but worked to cover it for her sake.

"Mother, I don't know that I can do this. I—"

She cut him off with a curt shake of her head.

"Matthew." Her voice was raised as loud as she ever allowed it—and it got his attention.

"Do not dishonor your family by continuing that thought. The exile was something that happened long before your father became king—you know that. You were born pure. You were born the son of a king. You will be king of the isles and the king of Triton."

Matthew tried to interject but she spoke over him.

"You *will* accept your birthright as those before you have—just as your father did."

Matthew watched emotion collect at the bottom of her brilliant blue eyes, stunned to silence at her iron response.

"Son, you have no idea the sacrifice that has been made to protect your position. I will not allow you to lose it through something so dishonorable and small as self-pity."

She was unmoving. And more emotional than he ever considered she would be. Matthew was concerned about disappointing her, but this reaction was one much beyond mere disappointment. This reaction looked more related to anger—or fear, maybe. He couldn't place it. He couldn't understand it. He didn't know from what deep reservoir it rose.

Matthew felt his mother's grip on his hand begin to loosen, not realizing how tightly she'd squeezed it during her discourse. He blinked in disbelief and tried to understand from where her reaction came. She seemed ready for his words—prepared almost. He wondered if she'd known his feelings already, maybe even for a long while. She was his mother, after all.

Even so, it surprised him to see her call vehemently for his silent and dutiful obedience to the subject. Matthew expected pushback, but he also expected compassion, empathy—some acknowledgement that his feelings would be considered.

But he received none of that.

He was only a breath away from questioning his mother on the details of her practiced response when a knock interrupted at the door. It was the housemaid.

"Beg your pardon, your grace. A young lady calls."

The maid bowed and left quietly. Matthew sighed his disappointment, dropping his head at the news. He raked back his blond hair with both hands and rested his forehead on his mother's lap.

"Go, my love," she urged.

She pushed his hair away from his face and nodded him out the door.

Matthew started his way down the wide marble hallway. The clack of his shoes against the floor reverberated off the walls and floated up to the arced ceilings, filling the empty spaces with distant echoes. The conversation with his mother felt unfinished and he dreaded the duty she called him to.

Regardless, he knew how to do this part. And he knew he had to do this part. His body did it robotically, without his needing to give it orders. His shoulders pulled back into their rehearsed, regal placement. His chin lifted higher, not too much, but just enough to place his status where it belonged and could be observed.

Duty. Not self-pity. Born for this. He repeated it over and over, but it was only a painted mask—plain and simple. And as feigned as his desire to be meeting another match.

Matthew opened the door to an ornamented tearoom where a woman sat waiting. She was more attractive than most he'd seen in these meetings, and undoubtedly the winner of the day. She was pure, with the lightest of yellow hair that fell like corn silk down her back. Her eyes were blue pools of crystal and her face rested beautifully like that of a doll—the fairest white, with faint pink highlights on her cheeks and lips. She sat upright on the edge of her seat, feet folded neatly below her, imperial in her every detail. She gave away nothing. No glimmer of emotion escaped her. She was well-rehearsed, indeed.

"Good evening," he greeted her.

She didn't stand.

"Your grace," she said evenly, unmoved.

He lifted his voice, suddenly offended by her. "Do you not stand in the presence of your prince?"

Even he was surprised he'd asked it. He didn't think he cared about such trivialities, but this was the first time it had ever happened, and it bothered him more than he knew it would.

The woman was sharp in her response, not angry, but direct, and with the slightest edge to her tone, deriving even more disquiet in him.

"Your grace, if we match, as they consider we may, will you require me to stand every time you enter a room for the rest of my life?" she asked.

"'If we match?'" he repeated briskly. "That's a fine arrogance you wear for our first meeting."

"It's a fine arrogance for you to require me to stand after never having met you at all," she retorted.

She was still calm and even in her responses, although unwavering in her bluntness.

"That is the very nature of royalty, girl, one does not question its worthiness, one stands simply because one is royal—"

He stopped cold in hearing his own words. This is exactly what he just told his mother he didn't want to be. Now he stood arguing over it with someone whom he happened to agree.

Matthew squeezed his face together and shook his head in disbelief at what he'd just said. He turned toward the woman to amend his words, but she was gone. He heard the large oak door shut from across the tearoom and looked around at the abandoned space before him.

She'd walked out on him.

It wouldn't stand. He had to correct it. He raced after her.

He had to let her know that he agreed with her. He couldn't believe he was running. He couldn't believe she'd walked out on him. He opened his mouth to call after her and realized he didn't know her name to call. He'd demanded she stand in his presence, but he didn't know her name.

There was a lot to regret about the interaction.

He pushed on the heavy doors that broke out to the night and felt the cold air spill into the castle. Snow fell in generous flakes and sparkled in the light from the lanterns that were fixed upon the stone diamond walls of the castle.

Matthew squinted through the snowfall to find the girl tying a cloak around her shoulders and readying herself to mount a horse. Her breath blew angry clouds into the air in front of her.

"Girl! Where is your escort? You don't intend to ride home in the dark, alone, in the snow."

She narrowed her eyes toward him, clicked her mouth, and in one smooth motion, led the horse into a swift, unhesitating gallop—away from the castle. Away from him.

CHAPTER TEN

FAITH

Faith rode briskly away from the castle and down the path to the gates that had led her in just a short half hour earlier. After waiting far too long for the short minute she spent with the prince, she was interested in feeling nothing but the snow melt into her hair and eyelashes. But she had one stop to make first.

She let her horse trot out through the gates and into the large, wooded area that surrounded the exterior walls of the castle. The land was beautiful and mountainous; always draped in the sound of the waves on the rocks just below them. She loved these islands, even with everything that came with them. The canopy of ancestorial pine trees covered the clouded sky above her and she was left with nothing but instinct to guide her back to the spot they'd chosen.

"Hodes?" she whispered.

She listened at the quiet stillness in front of her. Nothing but the soft fall of snowflakes filled the air. She dismounted; certain she was close. The crack of a stick behind her jumped her shoulders and turned her quickly around to face the noise.

"Hodes!" she exclaimed, sighing relief.

The limber, white-haired man toppled over with laughter, displaying no shame for the start he'd caused her. His cheeks were tinted with the life of cold air and his eyes sparkled against it.

"Did I get you?" he laughed.

She shoved him in the shoulder before giving into laughter herself. She couldn't help it. Ornery as he was, she loved him with all of her being. He was the only thing besides her horse she called a friend.

Hodes wasn't done yet. He mockingly prodded her.

"Back so soon from the meeting with the prince? It must have gone well."

His last sentence dripped with sarcasm.

"Ha, ha," she said dismissively.

Faith knew Hodes was waiting for more of a reply, but she also knew he wouldn't push her for it. He always respected whatever boundary she proffered. She untied her cloak as she pondered what to share. She carefully peeled off layers of the dress her mother had spent hours getting her into and handed each of them to Hodes delicately. She wouldn't risk tearing it and having to explain.

"He asked me to stand when he came into the room," she said dryly.

Hodes burst out laughing. "Oh, the poor devil."

He put a loving, paternal arm around her shoulders as they walked. "And how exactly are you going to explain this to your parents?"

"One problem at time, Hodes," Faith said.

She'd become tangled in one of the lace layers of the ensemble and was hopelessly tied up in it. Hodes moved to help her out of the web, and she smiled at him weakly, thankful for his steadfast presence at her side.

Faith knew, that Hodes knew, what would face her when

she reached home. The truth of her exchange with the prince would not be welcomed news. She'd been groomed for this one encounter—this one moment—for her entire life.

Her parents would not hear this story amenably. They would see a lifelong investment, forfeited on account of a child's foolish pride—her pride.

"Take your time getting home," Hodes offered gently. He whispered, "at least make it look like you were in his company for more than a few minutes."

Although Hodes spoke with assurance in his voice, Faith knew they shared concern over the unavoidable calamity that would come when her parents found out what happened. She would delay her return to the house as long as was possible.

"You're right." She looked around through the falling snow, choosing her path. "Meet you there later?" she offered.

Hodes nodded and held out a steady hand for her leg up.

"You bet," he said. He dipped his chin into her horse, clicked his tongue, and gave a soft pat on the back the steed's backside.

To Faith, there was nothing better than a beach ride at night, especially in the snow, and most especially when there was a need to escape the obligations that imprisoned her every day. She was thankful Hodes allowed her the freedom to do this alone. He wasn't supposed to, but he did it out of mercy— or pity. The personal risk he assumed by letting her go was great, but she treasured it and she respected him enough to be careful in her goings. Besides, they'd been at their little heists for far too long to stop now.

Hodes was there at her birth. To her parents, he was the hired help: the farm hand, the stable cleaner and fence builder. To Faith, he was a best friend, a mentor, a confidant, and a protector. The nearly four decades that separated them made him nearer a grandparent than a peer, but he was the one person she could always talk to. He was the one with whom she'd shared her crushes; to whom she expressed her frustrations and her dreams; and to whom she poured out her heartbreaks—most of which came by the hands of her parents.

Hodes had seen her at her best and seen her at her worst, and he remained beside her. To Faith it felt like Hodes was the only person who didn't require a performance from her—who didn't have mandatorily met expectations for her every breath. Most importantly, Faith knew that Hodes would be there even if she couldn't win the prince of the Diamond Isles—or any other match for that matter.

She wasn't sure her parents would feel the same.

To them, Faith felt as if she was nothing more than a bargaining chip—a chess piece. Every choice she could remember had been a political play to position her parents into Diamond Isles favor. They were one of the wealthiest families in the isles. They were among generations of pure lines on both her parents' sides and narrowly missed marrying into the royal family more than once.

That was a generational mistake Faith's parents aimed to correct. And it narrated every detail of her life from the earliest time she could remember.

After an hour pushing into the coast, Faith knew her horse was nearing his threshold. She also knew her parents would be nearing theirs. Obliged, she pulled the reigns in the direction of her home and donned her duty as she'd been taught.

Approaching the estate, she could see Hodes waiting in the usual meeting place just beyond the estate's visual line. He'd lit a small candle and propped it up on the stone next to him to light the words he read, immersing himself in another world, as usual. She saw him stir at her approach and shook her head in disbelief at how far away he could hear her coming. He didn't look for her. He simply stood and gathered his things, knowing she'd come around in a few short moments.

Faith felt Hodes' heavy hands as he placed them on her shoulders, and she listened to him sigh at the inescapable responsibility that set before her. He felt the burden as obliquely as she did, and she loved him for it.

"Okay," he said conclusively.

His hands tapped her shoulders once, twice, three times, and then he stepped out of her way.

She traded him the horse's reigns for the gown she re-donned, working on layer after layer. She could turn on the act with the strike of a match—it's what they'd taught her, after all.

She straightened, nodded to Hodes, and began the walk to the giant doors that crowned the estate. Through the windows, she observed her parents anxiously waiting by the fireplace, her father pacing, her mother not knitting the mess of yarn that lay unattended before her.

Faith took one last look up into the night sky above her, craning back her neck to let the snowflakes fall onto the skin of her face. As they melted, they turned to water and dripped off the sides of her cheeks like cold tears. They were the only tears she'd be allowed tonight, so she lingered for a moment longer, and then pushed open the goliath doors before her.

CHAPTER ELEVEN

JUDE

The Physis Sea

Jude pulled through choppy water with seven other crewmen from the Refuge. They strained against the sea as a machine, each part working toward the same end. As they came upon a pile of debris, one of the crewmen shouted over the noise, "life!"

Jude's eyes shot toward the direction his crewman pointed. The man in the water struggled to swim, using one good arm, the other missing just past his elbow, still fresh from its removal.

Jude was surprised the man was still conscious. He signaled the crew to paddle over and pull the injured man aboard. Jude strained against the oar with everything in him, exhausted from the last three days of rescues. He knew the crew was tired too. He could feel their fatigue in every half-awakened pull.

He'd lost count of how many they'd drawn from the water and delivered to the Refuge over the past few days, but he knew they were close to capacity aboard. They'd have to sail away from the fighting soon, and he was relieved for it.

Jude shouted to the man in the water, "ho there! We'll get you to safety! Can you raise your arm?"

The men lifted their oars from the water and shakily floated to the man through the wreckage. The injured man turned in the water to offer up his good arm, leaving him with what was left in his legs to keep his head above the hungry water.

Jude cleared room for the soldier in the skiff while two of the crewmen reached over its side to pull the man in.

Without warning, explosions blasted from the belly of a ship to their east. They hit nearer and nearer until the hits were upon them and the water rained upward, blinding Jude and the rest of the crew in an all-too-familiar shade of navy blue.

"Boom!"

Jude wiped water from his eyes while a laughing Chef Jackson came from behind him and patted him on the back jovially. He'd tossed a cup into the full sink of water in front of Jude.

"I got you!" he laughed, triumphantly.

"You know, Jackson," Jude said, smiling and wiping his face, "I could just leave you here to do all these dishes by yourself."

He poked Jackson with an elbow.

"Ah," Jackson quipped, "you'd never do that because I'm too awesome." Jackson sang his words more than he spoke them, common for people with his form of mutation.

Jude laughed and nodded his agreement. He couldn't help it. Jackson wore his extra chromosome well. What the rest of Physis considered a deformation, Zoarians knew to be valuable. Jackson was a skilled chef for their ragtag crew, even if he may be lacking in dish-washing fervor.

Chef Jackson rolled up his sleeves and started drying the dishes Jude positioned for him. This had become a routine for the pair in the days the Refuge was not pulling victims out of a fighting pocket.

After a few trips to the kitchen after hours, Jude started to genuinely look forward to the time spent beside his friend. Life was always a little easier—a little simpler—with Jackson around. It was part of what made people like him so necessary to the Refuge mission. He was a constant reminder of how much value each life held—regardless of territory, purity, or anything else.

"Hey, Jude." Jackson said. "Did you hear we're going home?"

Jude smiled, knowing Jackson wouldn't understand it was Jude, being the captain of the ship, who would have made that decision in the first place.

"I did, buddy." Jude smiled into the water. "I did hear that."

"Why do you think we're going home?" Jackson asked.

"Well, for one reason, I think we're all a little tired." Jude gave Jackson a sideways look. "Well, everybody except for you."

Jude passed him a cup to dry.

"And..." Jude drew this word out, not sure how much to share. "And, Miss Collette is nearly ready to have her baby, and I'd really like it if that could happen in Zoar, and not on the boat."

Chef Jackson placed the dried cup on top of Jude's head, balancing it there with careful precision.

"You know, we have lots of healers on this boat who can help her have her baby."

Jude bucked the cup off and into Jackson's victorious catch.

"Boom!" Jackson yelled again. "We're good at that," he stated proudly, safely returning the cup to its cupboard.

Jude laughed. "Yes, we are good at that, my friend."

Jude high-fived Jackson before handing him another dish.

He continued, "you're right. We do have a lot of healers, but Miss Collette and the baby will be safer in Zoar."

"Why's that?" Jackson asked plainly.

"Well, buddy, because not all of Physis is okay with the fact that Collette and I don't match."

Jackson nodded knowingly. "Kinda like me," he said, matter-of-factly, stating the observation while not marrying it to sentiment. "I don't match hardly anybody," he said lightly.

"Yeah," Jude nodded. "Kind of like you."

After a moment Chef Jackson's expression turned back to its animated nature and he held out his arms making a round shape over his midline.

"Man, it's like Miss Collette's got a watermelon under there."

Jackson filled his cheeks with air and exaggerated his arms in a generous circle.

Jude laughed and let the previous subject go with it.

"Yeah, don't tell her that, okay buddy?"

They laughed over the shared observation while Jackson wobbled around the kitchen with his invisible watermelon belly. Jude felt weight rise off his chest and resolved to enjoy the reprieve of levity with his treasured friend. It felt good to let some of the worry go, even if it was just for a moment.

Jude took a deep breath and enjoyed the ease of laughter, and while he did, he hoped one day the rest of Physis would know the gift of the humans they named mutants.

Days later, Zoar was finally within sight.

Collette had been racked with birthing pains for the last day and a half and relief washed over Jude when the horizon finally spotted with the first glimpse of Zoar. He'd never been so happy to see his home, and it seemed the rest of the crew shared the sentiment. They'd been gone for over two years.

Two years that, to Jude, felt more like ten.

Families and friends gathered on the docks at the coming ship. Natives must have watched for and recognized the Refuge sails because hordes of Zoarians surrounded the homecoming crew as they disembarked their sea vessel. Joyful embraces and delighted outbursts bubbled up from happy huddles in every available space around the ship.

But Jude missed it. He missed all of it. He had one urgent errand before any reunion could begin. With one arm firmly on Collette's back, he helped her from the Refuge, through the excited crowd, and up the hill—straight for Mae's house. Jude didn't know a lot about the baby birthing process, but he knew theirs was coming.

And fast.

CHAPTER TWELVE

JONATHAN

Zoar

Jonathan smiled weakly as he watched Jude lead Collette away from the crowd and up the hill to Mae's house.

Jonathan imagined this would be the first of many children from the pair. He couldn't help but think how lucky the child would be to have Jude and Collette as parents. He fought the instinct to run up the hill and help deliver the child, but he knew it would be better to let Mae do it.

She knew what to do.

Jonathan couldn't help but imagine, even if for the quickest of instants, what it would be like to be the man having a child with Collette today. He didn't host the thought for long. He pushed it out of his mind as quickly as he could gain control over it. Thought control was a challenge when it came to Collette, but he'd resolved not to dishonor his friend by thinking about his friend's wife.

He'd committed to it the day he watched them get married... and every day since.

THREE YEARS EARLIER

Jonathan stood next to Jude in the base pool of the main waterfall in the Western Bay. It was the centerpiece of the Western Bay, and it rang with unignorable command.

The water fell far behind them, but the mist of its majesty carried over in the wind with every breeze. The tenderness cooled Jonathan and helped ease him toward calm. He could tell Jude was nervous too. He watched as his friend rocked back and forth, shifting his weight from one foot to the other while his pulse thumped unhindered in the vein in the side of his neck.

Jonathan placed a hand on Jude's nearest shoulder. Of course, he was nervous. Who wouldn't be?

A few friends and family stood nearby, some choosing the water, some choosing the land on which to watch the proceedings. The sun was beginning its descent into the western horizon painting the sky in strokes of marvelous pastels. It was the only appropriate backdrop for such an occasion, and Jonathan admired it, thinking it was the most beautiful sight he'd ever seen.

Until Collette broke into his sightline.

Her hair had been delicately braided and laced with white, tropical flowers. The rest of it curled as it always did, most of the way down her back. She floated through the water toward them, a picture of exquisite beauty and graceful composure. The bottom of her dress rested elegantly on top of the water as she came toward them. Lilies grew up out of the water surrounding her in purple blooms and proffered a dreamlike picture to set behind one of the most moving things Jonathan had ever seen.

He felt Jude lean against him for balance, overcome, just as he was. Jonathan steadied him discreetly and let the scene consume him. He was allowed to watch the bride at a wedding. He was going to enjoy it. He'd studied healing side-by-side with Collette for years and she was now as she'd always been—all-consuming calm, just like the glassy water that surrounded her. Nerves or not, she didn't show them. She just moved forward, steady and sure—the picture of rest and assuredness.

It was there, standing next to his brother, listening to him pledge his love to Collette, and watching her look deep into Jude's eyes and vow the same... it was then that Jonathan promised himself he would no longer entertain the thought of he and Collette. At every instance where she came to his mind, he would escort the thought out as quickly as it came, little knowing how often that would be over the course of the next three years.

Jonathan gathered his personal effects from the Refuge. He'd deliver what Jude had left behind a little later. He was anxious to greet his own mother first. He hadn't seen Sarah for over two years, and it'd been two years too long.

Sarah was the only one who saw him give himself away at the wedding. Of course, his mother would be the one to see right through him. He should have known she would. He should have guarded his expressions more closely.

She'd confronted him about it afterward, asking every hard question a mother would, and challenging him in his intentions to work on the ward floor with Collette for the next few years on the mission.

Sarah warned him about what it would do to him. She told him it would become the haunting of his every day. She told him it would crush him. And she was right.

For most of his life, Jonathan thought his loyalty to Jude was the strongest thing he would ever feel, but over the last few years that loyalty had been challenged in ways he never thought possible. Collette was kind and empathetic; but smart and analytical too. She was funny, and beautiful, and she had a rare balance of strength and delicacy that made her femineity sing.

Now returning to land, the separation from her would take some getting used to, but Jonathan was relieved at the idea of getting off the ward floor for a while. He needed to not be working beside her day after day. Her presence *did* haunt him—just like his mother told him it would. His affection for Collette was his greatest burden, and now he could only cling to the hope that a new environment and a fresh routine would ease the ache, even if just a little.

One thing he knew, is that he owed Sarah an apology. He'd been short with her, dismissive of her words of warning. Even when he knew she rebuked him out of love and a desire to protect him, he'd shrugged her off, frustrated that she could see through him. Frustrated that he knew she was right.

She did what mothers do though, and even though he'd been dismissive, she'd come to see him off anyway, reminding him again and again of the love and pride she held for him.

Jonathan welcomed the opportunity to embrace her again. The comfort of the one who knows a soul better than any other—it was the life-saving salve that awaited him off the Refuge deck, and he was ready to sink into it. He stuffed his last remaining items into a bag and gave the ward floor a lingering, last glance.

"Jonathan."

A familiar voice sounded behind him.

He turned to find Mae standing at the door. Her hands were clasped in front of her like they always were, wrapped one over the other. Her short stature always took him by surprise. Standing over six feet himself, Mae barely made it up to his midsection, and yet somehow being this near her made him feel safer, as if she would be the one protecting him if it came down to it.

"Mae!" he embraced her with joy, already feeling relief from his reflections. "Ah, I've missed you! How is Collette—"

She cut him off before he could finish by placing an interrupting hand on his forearm. His words were stopped by her expression, which instantly became his sole focus.

He'd known Mae his entire life. He knew her well. And he knew, without a doubt, that whatever she said next was going to change his life forever.

CHAPTER THIRTEEN

MATTHEW

The Diamond Isles

Matthew sat one seat down from his father, forcing his expression to appear more alert than he was. He shifted his weight in the unforgiving chair below him and smothered a shiver that ran down his leg. The room held a chill that sunk into bones the moment one entered it. The ceiling was high, and it hung an iron bronze chandelier down from its center. The walls and floors were the same white marble and sparkling diamonds that covered the inside of the rest of the castle, but one wall in the meeting room was made entirely of glass. It looked out onto the frozen sea outside and leaked its cold up the diamond walls and into the room in which they gathered. Matthew watched white caps form and then disappear into the dark and wondered what hid under the surface of the sea.

He wondered if he could hide there too.

"Hm-hm." The king cleared his throat beside Matthew, pulling the prince's attention back to the meeting at hand.

The high officials of the Diamond Isles were bringing forth their meeting agenda items, one by one. Some were simply status updates on the goings-on of their respective areas. Others brought weightier requests or unresolved issues from previous sessions. Matthew had only recently begun sitting in on the proceedings but rarely paid attention long enough to feel anything but indifference at the information shared there.

Lacome was the last to speak and presented the royalty with the Diamond Isles' need for a more stable defense plan in case of attack. It was evident to Matthew that the king, and the others in the room, had heard this request many times before. He also noticed how readily the king dismissed the ask.

Matthew watched Lacome calculate his reply. He observed how carefully he controlled his breathing when the king continually cut him off, not allowing him to present the entirety of his argument. Lacome was making grand efforts to measure his response to the king. And though the king may not have noticed it, Matthew did.

Lacome didn't like the king—and he was struggling to contain it.

When Lacome was finally offered the chance to speak again, he did so directly, maybe hoping to get his point across before he was interrupted again.

"Your Grace, we have been aggressive in the offensive for a long while. We have acquired control over much land and many territories, but we have lost much as well. Our defense at home has never been thinner. I fear we are at risk—especially with the unrest on Tri—"

That was all the king would hear. He raised a hand for silence to which Lacome complied.

As far as Matthew could see it, Lacome was right. After what he had just experienced at Triton and what little fleet they had remaining on the Diamond Isles, Matthew could easily see the validity in Lacome's concerns. They needed to pull back from the war front and bring detachments home to guard the isles. And it would be an additional benefit to have reinforcements to address the growing unrest in Triton. Anyone could see it.

So, why was the king so readily dismissive? Other than his pride in the superiority of the isles, what reason could he have for declining such a request?

Matthew's contemplation must have been observable, because his thoughts were interrupted at the subconscious reception of his own name. He snapped alert to the conversation with apology.

"I'm sorry?" Matthew asked, having missed the question.

The king shook his head slightly, and smugly turned to his son to repeat Lacome's inquiry.

"The commander would like to know if, as a part of your training, you would like to weigh in on this."

Matthew slowly looked from his father to Lacome, who had picked up on Matthew's ambivalence. Lacome was the picture of composure, while Matthew felt the weight of the air between them in a crushing incumbrance. He did not have the years of practice Lacome had at this. This is exactly what Matthew had been trying to express to his mother just a week before. He wasn't ready for political games. He knew he was beat. He didn't agree with his father, but he knew disagreeing with the king in front of the high officials would be devastating to what was already an uneasy situation.

Lacome identified Matthew as attainable prey, and he'd struck with deadly accuracy.

Integrity or loyalty? Every person in every territory in Physis would choose loyalty as the more valuable ideal. But more and more Matthew thought they all might be wrong.

He chose quickly.

"How dare you defy me in front of the leaders?!"

The king's shouts reverberated off the marble in the study.

"Father, I didn't defy you."

Matthew sat in an upright chair while his father paced

angrily around the room.

"Silence is defiance! It's just as damaging as outright opposition and you know it!"

The king slammed his hands on the white desk before him. Matthew didn't respond. The silence that hung stagnant before them felt just as heavy as that which had stilled the room of leaders just moments ago.

Matthew sighed, knowing he wouldn't be released without explanation.

"I didn't speak because I didn't agree with you. I *don't* agree with you," he corrected. "We need a stronger defense and the only reason I can see for you *not* addressing it, is that you're too prideful to show what you think is weakness to the rest of Physis." Matthew lifted his shoulders. "Pulling back from the front would lend to the territories that we have a need. It would give us away, and I think you're too afraid to—"

The king started to reply, "how dare you—"

Matthew cut him off. "How dare I? Father, the residents of Triton literally throw food at you, and you question my actions?! We discuss what the other territories could do to us while just across the bay the people of Triton are ready to blast through our own castle walls!"

The king was silent at his words and Matthew took the opportunity to continue.

"Tell me father, why was Cleopas not here today presenting with the other high officials? Where is any representation from Triton?"

"You know why," his father stated, sharply.

"Say it. Tell me why Cleopas is not here."

The king sighed. "Matthew, it is the way of Physis. The exile happened long ago. Who am I to make my own rules for the land? And who are you to question them?"

Matthew was silent, unsure of how to respond. Duty and truth were at war within him, freezing his words.

The king broke his son out of their stalemate with one

defining, and all-too-familiar word.

"Leave."

Void of any other choice, Matthew submitted, ever surer that he would never agree to be the king of the isles.

CHAPTER FOURTEEN

FAITH

Faith sat on a stool in front of her mother, who delicately worked little braids into a bundle at the back of Faith's head. They'd done this hundreds of times, but Faith couldn't miss how much more careful her mother was this time. She felt her mother's hands tremble behind her as she worked through her thick golden cords of hair.

"You know what this would mean for our family." Her mother spoke to Faith as she worked.

"Yes, mother. I know."

Faith's mother yanked slightly on the braid she held, correcting Faith's response without using words of her own.

"Ow!" Faith protested.

"Sit up straight," her mother said poking her in the back.

Faith obediently straightened while her mother continued to coach her.

"Not only would it put our family in the highest position next to the royal family itself, but it could ensure our future for generations..."

Faith continued for her, having memorized the speech before her arithmetic.

"And it puts the isles in its most advantageous position. With our families' combined fortunes, the isles can acquire the loyalties that would take Agon once and for all."

Faith watched herself as she said it in the mirror, working on her expression, posture, and composure as she was taught.

"Very well," her mother said, finishing her hair. "Let's look at you."

Her mother backed up to give her the space to stand and then carefully inspected her life's work from top to bottom, appraising every detail down to the last stitch.

"Darling. It's beautiful." She sighed with satisfaction. "You are fit to be queen, without a doubt!"

As her mother marveled over her work, a maid came to the door of Faith's bedchamber.

"Mr. Hodes has arrived with the horses and carriage."

The maid smiled admiration at Faith. Faith could only imagine what story the maid may have been told about Faith's last visit with the prince. She was likely dreaming up her own fairy tale version of what the next few hours would be like for Faith, though she had no idea what the last had exposed.

The truth was that the maid didn't know what transpired the last time Faith visited the icy castle. Nor did she know what the prince was really like in person. No one knew. No one but Hodes. And friend that he was, he hadn't let loose of her secret, or tipped anyone off that he had information they did not.

When the crisp invitation arrived so soon after their last visit, the household assumed success, and Faith didn't dream of correcting them. The vague answers she'd offered the night she returned seemed to suffice. Maybe her parents excused her ambiguity out of a delusional hope of her swooned innocence. Faith wasn't sure how long they'd let her continue her silence without requiring more details about the interaction with the prince. She'd only hoped they would leave her long enough for her to compose a believable story.

Then the invitation arrived.

The rich script on white parchment, paired with the light blue, shining seal of the royal family was unmistakable... and an odd relief to Faith. It sent the household into a frenzy of glee and placed an ill-set balance of release and dread freshly into Faith's lap.

Her father was waiting out front with Hodes and the carriage when she arrived, her mother glowing in the hue of her great work on display beside her. An all-too-invested household staff stood in a line of invisible salutes to gawk at her departure, hardly concealing the delicious possibility of having royal affiliations themselves. Her mother continued to spout off instructions—instructions she'd repeated since the day Faith could understand them.

"Keep up your posture, dear. And don't cross your legs, you're not a barn boy. Excuse yourself at a quarter past to check your face and hair. Don't lick your lips and don't fidget with your gown. Keep your gloves on so you don't pick at your nails and..."

Faith stopped listening as she approached the carriage. Both her father and Hodes removed their hats and smiled at her with pride.

"That poor man," Hodes said to her, shaking his head. "He don't stand a chance, darlin'."

Faith allowed the slightest grin for him and accepted her father's hand to climb up into the carriage. She took her place in the back and turned to face her father and mother, who stood side by side at its door.

"We have a lot invested in the success of this match, Faith." Her father looked stern, seriousness overcoming his pride. "This is more than a meal. This is business, and we need you to perform well. You represent more than yourself," he said in admonition.

"Yes, father," she replied nervously. "I'll do well."

Faith looked into the faces of her parents, the picture of anticipation and fear. She resented that she was nothing more than a bargaining chip to them, but it didn't stop her stomach from wrenching into a ball at the hope to fulfill their expectations. She didn't want to let them down. No matter how much she didn't care to be with the prince.

With a dutiful smile, she leaned forward to tap the door and watched as the horses jerked the carriage forward, pulling her to her future—whether she wanted it or not.

Faith sat across from Matthew in the back acres of the royal estate. Pines grew tall all around and were dressed in white tips of the morning's snow. An ornate table was set before them, positioned in the middle of a garden of sparkling lion statues made from the same diamond stone of the isles. They were shadowed by the great canopy of pines which were old enough to have seen centuries more than the two of them.

This time when the prince arrived, Faith promptly rose from her seat out of both due respects, and the fear of causing a similar quibble as before.

The prince did not remark on it.

He came swiftly in, took his place at the table, and sat in silence for ten minutes. He shifted every few minutes, playing with a utensil or fiddling with something on his shirt or the tablecloth, but never looking up: never speaking.

In the silence, she'd considered several things to say, but she knew the protocol. She knew not to speak unless he did. And she wasn't going to risk doing something as offensive as the last time. So, she sat in silence, knowing she honored her training by doing so.

After another ten minutes had passed, Faith was consider-ing politely leaving, unsure of what other options existed. She knew it wasn't the choice her parents would have preferred, so to keep herself in the chair, she let her mind drift to the expectations and questions that would await her when she returned home. She pictured the desperation she'd seen in her parents' faces as they closed the door to her carriage, and of the maid who would have given anything to trade places with her today.

While contemplating the gravity of the outcome of the awkward picnic, her thoughts were interrupted by the prince's sudden stirring. He pushed himself to the edge of his chair and placed his elbows on his knees, leaning closer to her. He rubbed his hands together and breathed clouds of warmth into the cold air between them. He lifted icy blue eyes to the space behind her and stated his question at the empty space, more a command than an inquiry.

"Shall we ride."

Acres of forest and mountains passed over and under them before the prince slowed his horse to a trot. He pulled reigns up to a tree he seemed to know well. The roots of it grew up out of the ground, creating a nest under it. He dismounted and showed his horse to a freshwater stream that flowed through a break in the snow. Familiarity dressed the prince in the smoothness of the routine. This was not the first time he'd been here.

It was then, for the first time since she'd arrived, that the prince turned his attention on her. He looked up at her with the brilliance of sapphire in his eyes and offered her a hand to dismount. Once upon the ground, the prince laid his overcoat under the cozy tree as a makeshift blanket and offered her a seat, leaning against the grand upward-grown roots.

After sitting himself, he finally spoke. "I wanted to offer you my apologies for how I spoke to you at our last meeting. I was- "

She cut him off, regretting it immediately, but it was too late to retreat, "No, I'm sorry. It's my duty to stand in the presence of royalty and—"

This time he cut her off.

"You interrupt me so *you* may apologize?! Is your apology worth more than mine? It's as if you've no graces at all. How do they expect you to be a match for royalty?"

His tone was smug and proud, mocking her training in ways that would make her mother recoil in shame. The thought should have made Faith wither with concession, but it didn't. It made her mad.

"Ugh!" She groaned.

She rolled her eyes and stood, pushing off the tree behind her and away from him and snagging the lace on the sleeve of her gown. She yanked it away unapologetically and strode through the snow away from him. She could feel heat rise into her cheeks despite the cold of the air. She lifted the skirt of her gown higher and pulled the bottom of it up from her feet so she could move away from him faster.

"Where are you going?" he shouted behind her. "You don't know the way!"

She kept walking, indifferent to direction or destination. She just wanted to be rid of the expectations that ordered her every moment and entire existence. Walking away from the prince wouldn't make them go away, but in this moment, she couldn't find it in her to care for proper graces.

Faith could hear the prince yelling behind her but didn't respond. How he could ruin a moment so quickly! She heard surf in the distance and pushed toward it. At least the waves would make sense, even if nothing else did.

"Hey!" he called.

She was surprised he was still following her—still trying at all. She exhaled disgust at the thought of him and pushed toward the sound of waves getting closer.

"Hey!" he shouted again.

Faith could hear the prince closing the gap between them and picked up her pace. His pursuit may have been his own, but by it, she felt the pressure of everything everyone else expected of her. She was the pinnacle of hope for her household—and for the isles, as far as her mother and father were concerned. The weight of that responsibility sat heavily on her chest. Her lungs struggled against the cold, dry air, and the corset that wrapped and held her middle. She fought for a full breath while she moved but couldn't fill her lungs enough to satisfy her need. When the tree line finally fell away, it broke to open air in front of her and she groaned relief.

Faith found herself not on the shore of a rocky beach as she expected, but high above the surface of the icy water, on a cliff towering above waves that crashed against the diamond's solid walls below her.

"Hey!" the prince called again.

Faith turned against the voice of the prince behind her, and under the weighted pressure of expectation and the wild abandon that pushed against the ropes around her chest, she took two great strides, and leapt for the water below her—gown and all.

CHAPTER FIFTEEN

MATTHEW

"What?" Matthew said out loud.

He froze in astonishment and spoke to the empty air beside him. He couldn't believe it. He knew he may have been off-putting, but he had no desire to push the girl to a death jump.

"Hahaha!"

He heard laughter from below. Matthew ran to the edge of the cliff and peered over the great, sparkling wall below him.

"What?" he repeated out loud.

The girl splashed happily in the water below, giggling her delight at the dance she did with the waves. He couldn't help but smile. It disarmed him. Whether out of relief or befuddlement, he was intrigued by the beauty of the wild creature that had just plummeted herself off the wall in order to escape him.

Deep in the pit of his stomach stirred a new feeling—unsettling but somehow welcome all at once. It felt as though a candle had been lit and started to glow into his darkest places. He wanted to capture it. The newness of it was startling and it was something he did not want to miss. He wondered how one could capture and keep something so seemingly intangible. It seemed elusive, like he could lose it all in one quick instant.

So, he did the only thing he could think to do to preserve it.

He jumped too.

He gulped in as much air as he could and went running off a cliff he'd only ever thought to walk by. It was adventure unrealized, until the day she led him by leaping from it.

Matthew pushed hair from his right eye.

"Matthew," he said resolvedly.

She looked at him, questioning.

"Please, call me Matthew," he said.

She smiled at him hesitantly and offered a small nod.

After hitting the water and finding a slippery path back, Matthew built a fire as best he could, and pulled out the food that had been packed for them. The flames were dying down now, losing their warmth far too quickly. He looked at her, waiting, but she didn't offer anything.

After a moment, he gave in.

"And...?" he drew it out, letting her know he was annoyed. "What may I call you?"

She laughed her response at him. "I knew you didn't know my name."

He watched her, observing the ease of her laugh and the comfort with which she seemed to exist. She was a beauty. His first reaction was to take offense to her casual response but watching her try to stifle her laughter softened him past insult.

"Faith," she said when her laughter died down. "My name

is Faith."

He nodded, gazing into the last light of the fire before them. He knew he would only ever have to hear it once. He'd never forget it.

"Faith," he said, acclimating it to his mouth. "Well Faith, not only is that the first time a woman has run away from me, but it is also the first time a woman has jumped from a cliff to escape my presence."

He noticed how she smiled at this, seeming almost proud at the thought. She didn't raise her eyes from the sandwich in front of her and she didn't offer him a response.

"Oh, how am I going to explain this to my father?" Matthew wondered out loud.

Faith straightened at his words, suddenly serious.

"No, please," she begged.

She had a desperation in her voice. It was the first time she seemed anything but perfectly self-assured and confident to Matthew.

"Please," she said again, "don't tell the king. My parents cannot find out I did that!"

He nearly laughed at her expression but stopped when he saw the earnestness in her eyes—or was it fear? It was in that moment, for the first time, that Matthew considered what she must be going through. The match would be vital for any family trying to marry into royalty. Before, he'd only ever thought families would consider it a privilege to marry in, but the fear in her eyes told him a different story. It was one he hadn't contemplated before.

"Oh, no," he corrected softly. "No, don't worry. I won't tell."

He watched her relax and she nodded her gratitude weakly before half-heartedly returning to her food.

He spoke again. "It must be a lot of pressure to be put up for a match with a royal." He thought, and then carefully corrected himself. "Well, to be put up for a match with anyone,

I guess."

She stopped picking at her sandwich and looked up at him.

"It is," she conceded. "But the same for you, it must be hard to choose between so many." She paused, and then added, "well, no, your position is much easier." She smiled wryly. "Actually, I may not feel any regret for you at all, your grace."

This time he laughed too, appreciating her blunt-force candor. It wasn't often someone was so willing to speak freely to him. Oddly enough, it felt exciting to know she wasn't afraid to offend him. Apparently jumping off the cliff had done what he needed it to do, because the candle in the pit of his stomach was burning fire into him from the inside out. It was a discomfort he did not want to lose.

"No," he answered, "I suppose you wouldn't."

After another contemplative bite, he added, "I wonder though if I could earn your pity by telling you that someone threw food at me last week. And I don't mean a congenial food fight in the kitchen, I mean an all-out pelting of food and rocks."

"No!"

She covered her opened mouth in shock, and he nodded his affirmation of the statement. An hour later they remained under the same tree, next to the same dying fire, swapping stories of the pressure they experienced in their own respective ways. The snow had begun to fall again, softly, steadily decorating the world around them. They shared stories of inherited expectations to fit into lives they had not chosen. It was the first time in as long as he could remember that Matthew did not feel alone. He found himself wondering if she was drawn to him the way that he was to her. She was delicate and lovely, but she didn't blush at him the way women usually did. She didn't shy away from his eyes, but she took them boldly with hers when she spoke, almost like they were hers from the start. He didn't know what made her so comfortable, but he knew he wanted it. It seemed she was just as imprisoned as he was, but she lived with far more courage than he did, taking her prison walls and pushing them outward to their limits. It was unknown to him, and it both exhilarated him and terrified him at the same time.

Only one thing was clear. He wanted to see her again. And again, and again, he expected.

The sound of urgent hooves on the dirt broke them out of their collective spell and drew their attention to a rider from the castle. Matthew was being called back.

The queen would not make it through the night.

Matthew sat next to his mother's bedside unwilling to comprehend the reality before him. He knew she'd been declining, but no one told him the end would come so soon. He wasn't ready.

But he wouldn't have a vote in the matter. He was losing her. Right now.

By the time he'd ridden back to the castle and rushed to her side, it was too late to have any words with her. Her breathing was labored and uneven, her eyes were closed, and her movements minimal. When Matthew took her hand, she moved her head to his side and lifted her chin ever so slightly, noting his presence beside her.

Matthew looked from his mother to his father, who stood across from him. The king held his mother's other hand, pain drowning him from head to toe. Matthew knew this would be the most devastating loss the king would ever endure. Although he and his father were very different, they had always shared one thing in common—an immoveable love for the woman before them. It was the singular piece of common ground under their feet.

How would they manage in her absence? Matthew feared

not only for the future of his relationship with his father, but for the future of the isles. His father's rule was ruthless even when it was tempered by the presence of a kind and gentle woman beside him. She balanced the king's responses and challenged him on every decision.

What would he be like without her? How would he rule when he was tormented by grief?

Matthew didn't cry when she took her final breath. He just sat next to her, stroking her hand, unable to move from beside her. An hour later, everyone had departed but Matthew and his mother's maid. His head lay on the bedside, his mother's hand swallowed in the two of his.

"Prince Matthew?"

The maid spoke from behind him. He lifted his head to acknowledge her. As he did, she approached with a letter, sealed with the queen's mark.

"The queen asked me to give this to you after she passed."

The handmaid then took her leave, leaving Matthew alone with his mother's last words to him.

Matthew looked from the letter to his mother, and then back to the letter. Her handwriting artistically scribbled his name on the front of the envelope, and he touched it tenderly, remembering the beauty of his mother with a pen. He broke the seal slowly and lifted out the single square that was held within it.

In her unique hand, she'd written only one word. It was alien to him, completely unknown. But it was one that would change everything he had ever known.

"ZOAR"

CHAPTER SIXTEEN

MAE

Zoar

Mae stood in the kitchen drying dishes from their breakfast. Her heart was fuller than it had been, but it still sagged heavy with grief.

It was still hard.

Every morning the sun came up over the eastern sea, she searched down the hill, finding Sarah's porch swing with her eyes still expecting her to be in it. Every morning since she could remember, she peered out through that same creaky screen door to watch for her friend, swinging back and forth in rhythm with the dawn's tide, watching their shared sun climb into the expansive sky. And Mae knew that moments thereafter, after the sun climbed just high enough to make the water sparkle, the door would creak open, and knock shut, and she would need the table set for the of two of them; which then became the four of them; which then returned to just the two of them.

Just she and Sarah.

She knew death was a part of life, as inevitable as a day's end. Still, she didn't expect to be setting her kitchen table for one. She expected to be the one who would leave first.

Mae and the others on the council had worked it over and over with the island's healers. There was no getting around it. The fever that killed Sarah and so many others was introduced to Zoar through a soldier. One who had been scooped from angry seas and healed of his wounds, and then shipped to Zoar to finish his recovery. It was an experience shared by many.

The solider was helped to the island's infirmary, and inadvertently shared his fever with more people than anyone knew until it was much too late. Zoar was infected with the fever from the inside out, and Sarah was one of the last to give in to it.

Mae knew it was the Refuge that sent the injured man to the island. So, it was the Refuge that sent the fever to the island. All the council knew. She'd begged them to keep it quiet. What would happen if the rest of the island found out? What would the consequences be for the two men she loved the most in the world? She'd already lost her husband and dearest friend. What additional loss could this bring? What additional loss could she withstand?

Forget what the Zoarian natives would do to Jude and Jonathan if they found out, the guilt the crew would bury themselves under would be more than enough. It would not only end the Refuge mission, but it would destroy their spirits in the meantime.

The mission had brought Sarah to her death. And not just Sarah, but hundreds of others.

Mae remembered feeling relieved when Sarah's fight was finally over. It lasted weeks. It was valiant; but it was pitiful. And in the end, death was mercy.

How would she explain that to Jonathan? He'd received the news bravely, as any soldier would. He'd always been more composed than Jude, more able to control his emotions, more stoic, more noble, more steady. It's what made him a good healer.

Mae foresaw that he would swallow his emotion in the moment. That's not what worried her. It was the weeks and months that followed... those would be the true test to his grief.

It'd been a month since the Refuge returned and here, she was, checking Sarah's porch swing again, fully expecting her to be pushing back and forth on her swing. And she expected to see Jonathan footing about the porch in his strong and silent way, bending over his mother with a steaming cup in each hand, one for the both of them.

But she wasn't. And he wasn't.

He still wasn't.

Mae, Jude, nor Collette had seen or heard from Jonathan since the day they'd disembarked, and today was the last day Mae was willing to wait. As she contemplated her choices of action, Jude approached from his bedroom trying to shake the permanent, new-father tired from his face.

"Hey mama," he said easily.

She watched him as he bent to kiss her cheek and noticed the comfort with which he moved. She observed peace and lightness about him, so different from his last months on Zoar before they left for the mission. Purpose had found him; and in more ways than one. She was thankful to have him back, physically, of course, but even more so in spirit. He was himself again. He was different—more full, more colorful, and more worn. But also, more grown. It was him again, and it brought her incalculable pleasure.

"Have you heard from your brother?" she asked.

"No." His tone changed enough for her to know it bothered him too. "You?" he asked.

She shook her head. The baby cooed from the porch while Collette spoke to her, gently coaxing the sweet sounds out of her beautiful bronze baby. Mae and Jude watched together from behind the scenes, Collette oblivious to her audience.

Mae observed with maternal pride. "She took to motherhood like a duck to water, didn't she?"

Jude sipped coffee with a smile, nodding his agreement.

Mae remembered the weeks of waiting for Jude to tell her he'd fallen in love. Mae was not surprised, based on the patterns of his behavior for the months before the announcement, but once he told her, she knew it was right. He was like a ball of putty when it came to Collette, and Mae didn't think anything would ever melt him quite like that again.

But she could not have been more wrong.

The moment Mae put his baby girl in his arms she could feel his very world shake before him. With a wife and baby he adored, Mae wondered if Jude would ever leave Zoar again—if he'd ever relaunch the Refuge mission. The three different colors the little family represented would not allow for many safe places in the rest of Physis. It was a reality that would be a mission all its own. A mission much closer to Jude's heart than that of the Refuge. But whether Jude would or wouldn't relaunch the mission was a decision that would be waiting down the line. It was a bridge they'd cross when they came to it. Right now, she had to fill him in on what else had happened in the wake of their departure. As they watched Collette play with the baby, Mae carefully considered how to begin.

"Old Terrance Benjamin always used to tell me that parenthood was all about learning how to let your child go."

Jude smiled at her. She imagined he had fond memories of the old man who had introduced him to the sea.

Mae continued, "when you left on the Refuge, it was one of the proudest days, and one of the hardest days, of my life." She paused, trying to manage rising emotion at the memory. "It was a noble thing you wanted to do." She smiled at up her son recounting it. "I will never forget the first person who came in having been saved by the Refuge. He was a solider from Racham. He'd lost most of a leg when an explosion hit the side of his ship. He woke up in the infirmary of the Refuge and told us he'd been tended to by a tall guy with tattoos and dreadlocks and muscles too large to be a doctor's." Mae laughed, "you should have seen the pride in Sarah's face." She looked up into Jude's dark face and smiled. "I imagine I looked about the same."

Jude's heavy arm came around her shoulders as they stood watching Collette play with the baby.

"Jude, what you guys have done, what you've started—it's more than what you know." She paused, approaching carefully. "After you left, more ships launched with similar missions. They saw what you did, and they organized to do the same."

"What?" He turned to face her fully. She could see the hope in his eyes. "This is great! We can save so many lives like this. We needed so much help out there- ".

She saw inspiration spark in him as he spoke, and she cut him off before he could get too far ahead. She placed a hand on his forearm.

"Love, yes, it *is* great. The power of mercy is undeniably contagious and it's miraculous to see how one idea—your idea—has spread across the island, but it's also come with a cost." She faced him directly and chose her words carefully. "There have been discussions at council about the island's capacity to continue to take the refugees."

She saw his eyes narrow, pinching the skin above his nose. She knew he wouldn't like it. She didn't like it either.

"I don't want you to worry just yet, nothing has been decided about how to proceed, but I want you to be aware that this is a concern for the future of the island."

She watched him immediately begin analyzing, thinking through any possible solution. She was careful to leave out all the implications of their choice. It was too early for them to know. The grief was too fresh.

Mae waited in the silence before continuing. She wanted

him to leave knowing the truth of just how proud she was. Their decisions did have consequences, but they'd saved hundreds of lives in the meantime. It was a balance that required itself to be counted.

"Jude, what you have done is nothing short of miraculous. You created a crew out of nothing. You put a purpose in front of them—a purpose some of them will only ever know because of your mission. And you led them to save hundreds of peoples' lives—lives that represent virtually every territory in Physis."

She held his face with maternal tenderness. "You have so much to be proud of. Every choice comes with a cost, and the cost we face now, is that Zoar has never had more people coming to its shores. And people require resources—especially injured people. We're low on beds in the infirmaries; we're at capacity in the stay houses." She shrugged her shoulders in defeat. "We're even discussing turning parts of the school-houses into makeshift housing for those well enough to not need tending." She shook her head. "Consider food and medical supplies..." she trailed off seeing the recognition in his expression. "I expect we will have to vote on responsive plans in the coming months. I need you to be ready for it."

She hoped giving him this kind of warning would level his reaction when it happened, knowing he'd need time to work it over. She hoped that his growing family would reorder his priorities and inform a more tempered response than he may typically have. There was a lot more for him to consider than there was two years ago when they first pushed off from Zoar's shores.

The rocking chair creaked an interruption as Collette rose from it with the baby. She entered the kitchen wearing the morning sunshine in her expression.

"Who's up for a walk?" she proposed, drunk with the dawn and her new infant.

Mae rubbed Jude's arm and said determinately, "you go.

There's a visit I need to make."

Not long later, Jude, Collette, and the baby left out the front door, and Mae went out the back.

It was time to have a conversation with her other son.

CHAPTER SEVENTEEN

JONATHAN
ONE YEAR EARLIER

The Physis Sea

"I'm not doing it."

Collette looked Jonathan right in the eye, unmoved. They stood huddled together, whispering so the patients wouldn't overhear their conversation. Jonathan had seen this look in her eyes before and he knew he couldn't win. Collette's strong-willed stubbornness had become that of legends on the Refuge. He narrowed his eyes at her, considering his next move.

"Okay doc," he started, "I propose we resolve this the only way civilized people can." He paused and straightened and stuck out both his hands. "Rock, paper, scissors."

She sighed, "fine."

They positioned themselves for the battle, and at the strike of three, Jonathan threw what he knew would likely lose. Sharp as she was, while playing Rock, Paper, Scissors, Collette had a tendency to play the same every time. It made her easy to play around—and easy to play into. The hard part was letting himself beat her. As much as he didn't want to bathe the handsy and delirious Quartermaster Aegeus, he'd take the loss to see the triumphant smile spread across her face.

Collette smugly handed him a bucket at her victory. "You know where the sponges are doctor." She smiled and tilted her head to the side. "Or shall I call you, Martha?"

In his delirium, Quartermaster Aegeus was convinced the person bathing him was his old lover Martha, and things got tricky quickly. In truth, it was more uncomfortable for Jonathan to watch the quartermaster grope at Collette than it was to take it himself. Bathing the man was far from his favorite task, but it was the lesser of the evils as far as he could see it.

A few rows of patients away, batting briskly at the quartermaster's advances, Jonathan stole a glance back at Collette, happily rinsing tools and restocking the medical supplies.

"Worth it," he thought.

ZOAR

Clanging from the kitchen pulled Jonathan from his memory. Torturous as it had been to be working side-by-side with a woman he couldn't love, there were moments he wished they were back on the Refuge, tending patients and laughing at little things that made his days great. His constant dreams kept his thoughts away from the loss of his mother and sprinkled his subconscious with elusive contentment.

It was weird place to exist, nowhere and somewhere all at once.

Jonathan squeezed his eyes in protest at the light coming in through the window. The noise from the kitchen echoed in his head and pounded against his ears. While trying to stand, he knocked over the bottles he'd emptied over the last few weeks and sat back down to a spinning room. His head ached, his body was stiff, and he couldn't decide if he was hungry or if instead, he was going to vomit.

The smell coming from the kitchen made up his mind quickly. It was more than enough to straighten him and carry him toward it. The smell was the only indication he needed to know who'd come to visit. There was really no question to it at all.

"Take a seat," Mae said to him.

It was a little grimmer greeting than he'd expected. Her voice was low and even, stern almost. She pointed her chin in the direction of the table behind her, where a place was already set for him.

He was too hungry to do anything but obey. She filled the plate before him and said grace over it like she had every day of his life until he left for the Refuge. His hunger overcame him, and he cleaned the plate in front of him twice before she spoke again. She'd always been careful with timing, and he was beginning to think there may be something to it. Her narrow, dark eyes targeted his and held them steadily.

"It's not something you ever get used to—losing someone you love," she said it matter-of-factly, not clothing it with the empathy he'd expected. "I'm not going to tell you it's all going to be okay—it's going to hurt for a good, long time." She laid her small hand on his arm. "But honey, I need to remind you that you are not the first person on Zoar to lose someone."

There it was. It was the truth she was so famous for delivering.

"Son, most folks here have lost far more than a few people along the way. And can I remind you that most people on this island have never even known their true mothers?"

She was right. Jonathan was one of the only people on Zoar who was born to the parent he knew.

"You had it good, baby. You still do." She tapped his arm and pointed up to her house. "There's a house full of people up that hill who love you and miss you." Her yellow skin glowed with the light of the morning, and her eyes twinkled in anticipation of her last sentence for him. "And there's a beautiful baby girl up there who can't wait to meet you."

Jonathan's eyes shot up her words. "A girl?" he asked softly. It was the first time he'd spoken out loud in weeks and his voice croaked with under-use.

Mae squeezed her mouth upward. "She's perfect."

Jonathan looked from the house up the hill to the table below his hands. The realization of his situation washed over him again. Not his child. Not his woman. Grieving the loss of his mother.

Mae adjusted herself in her chair. She always knew more than she let on. "We all lose people we love, honey. Some who were ours to love. Some who were *never* ours to love." She patted his arm under her hand. "It's devastating both ways."

Mae pushed back from the table and brushed off her skirt. "You are the only one who can choose how you continue. Live with what you have left, or don't." She pointed around at the empty bottles that surrounded them. "But I'm not putting up with this a moment longer. And Sarah wouldn't either."

He nodded slightly while she cleared his empty plate from the table. She dropped them in the sink with the rest of the dishes from the meal she'd made and delivered her final remark.

"Take a shower and clean this place up."

And as she crossed the threshold she added, "I love you."

CHAPTER EIGHTEEN

MATTHEW

The Diamond Isles

Matthew didn't think about it long.

It felt like the first decision in a long time—maybe even in his entire life—that felt perfectly easy, perfectly right. There was no hesitation, no second-guessing, no stopping to think. He penned a letter to Faith in just under a minute and left it with the housemaid to deliver. She was the only one who knew where he was going, and Matthew knew she'd be faithful to deliver the message to Faith in the greatest confidence. It was a simple message, and direct.

> *Faith,*
> *I have to go for a while, but you are... extraordinary.*
> *Write me if you like.*
> *- Matthew*

It wasn't poetic, but he hoped it would communicate his message well enough. The evening air pushed in on him while he waded his way out of the royal estate. He didn't want to cause a stir, so he left on foot, knowing he would not return the horse anyway. He couldn't remember a time in his life when he'd felt so alive. It wasn't until he'd departed the royal grounds that he realized part of what was overcoming him was fear.

His insides shook with the chill in the air, and he started to notice prolonged stares from strangers here and there, extending their observations of him longer than would be normal. He hadn't spent enough time outside the castle walls to know what was typical, and his ignorance of common life suddenly felt like the great vulnerability it was.

He'd donned a hat and a stall boy's uniform to disguise himself, but he knew his pure features would be hard to miss— especially once outside the Diamond Isles. It would be a constant challenge to disguise himself, and one he had only ever imagined until now. Flashbacks of the volatile visit to Triton flooded his mind and quickened his heart rate as he made his way to the docks. He was somewhat unfamiliar with the route, having only travelled it by escort, and the features of his environment grew more foreign with every second. Still, the further he traveled from the castle, the more he felt it was the right choice—the only choice—for him.

He'd have to travel to Triton in order to pick up an export barge that would travel the greater distance out of the area. He would need to find a Diamond Isles & Triton vessel shipping exports to more distant islands if he was going to end up on one headed in the direction of Zoar. Upon investigation, Matthew had found the little island was as far away as one could get in Physis. It and the isles occupied opposite ends of their existence. He would have to move carefully and choose carefully if he was going to make the trip without being identified.

He pushed the creeping doubts from his mind. He thought of the freedom with which Faith seemed to live. This was his chance to leap from his own cliff, and he had to take it.

He ducked behind the corner of a building and urged his ears to catch the conversation between the fisherman and what appeared to be an isle footman, or chef maybe. The two animatedly bartered over prices until landing on a mutually amenable number and shaking gloved hands over it. It was clear the fisherman was a recessive and would be headed back to Triton for the night.

At least, Matthew hoped that's where he was headed.

He doubled back behind the building to the aft of the departing vessel, and with a soft jump from the dock, he was boarded and hidden behind crates of crabs before the fisherman was any the wiser. He exhaled his first triumph, letting new confidence sink into his skin.

This already felt like the right choice. Now, he was even more sure.

A short ride later, the dark shapes of Triton peaks shaded the night sky and Matthew discreetly slinked off the back of the boat and onto the aged docks of the mainland. His heart raced with the thrill of his covert adventure, so he intentionally slumped and forced his gait to slow. With one hand, he tipped his hat at a passerby like he'd seen the horsemen do on their routes at the castle. With his other hand, he held the bag he'd brought along. It held food, coin, and paper to write Faith—and maybe, eventually, his father. He didn't know what he would say when it was time, but he knew the time might come... one day. He wondered how the king would react when he found his son missing. He wondered how Faith would react.

His eyes scanned the boats lining the dock. Nearly all of them Diamond Isles & Triton vessels, easily identified by the large block letters painted on their port sides. What was harder for Matthew to determine was where each was headed and how to sneak his way onto the right one. After declining a few rows of possibilities, he spotted one loading for departure.

Several men formed a line carrying wooden crates from land to the ship, marching up and back along the gangway like ants in a line.

This was it.

He stuffed his bag into the back of his pants, so his arms were free of burden. He tucked his exposed hair back under his hat and joined the line of men carrying supplies aboard. His heart pounded as he approached the gangway, but no one stopped him. He kept his eyes down and followed the feet in front of him up the plank and onto the deck of the barge. He dropped the crate near the rest of them and looked around for a place to stow away. His eyes found a corner of the barge he thought would work, but as he started that way, one of the men behind him called out.

"Yo there!"

Matthew stopped in his tracks and turned to look at the shipman.

"There's more to be carried ya' lazy rat! Back in line, you will, or there be no port for yas."

"Right away, sir," Matthew said, immediately regretting it.

Matthew saw the shipman pause at the formal response he'd offered. The shipman grimaced, mouthing Matthew's words back at him like they were spoiled ale in his mouth. Matthew fell back in line, bearing another crate. He could feel the shipman behind him observing more carefully than before. Matthew kept his head down and said nothing. He loaded crates until they were all aboard and then followed the men to the pub to eat. He pulled off as the rest of the group entered, knowing he couldn't continue his pretense through the entirety of a meal. He had to find a way aboard now, while the rest of the crew was distracted.

Matthew nonchalantly walked in the direction of the outhouse and waited until no one was looking before redirecting toward the gangway. He quickened his pace when a few of the men came out to smoke around the fire, but they took no notice of him. They just rubbed their cold hands in front of the blaze and drank for numbness.

Matthew carefully plotted his way back through the street, ducking when he needed to. After a few close calls, he made it back onto the ship without being seen and feverishly looked for a place to hide.

He'd have to find a way to blend in. He'd have to merge into the natural flow of the crew. He tried out a spot above deck, but it was too inconspicuous. It wouldn't hide him for long and the trip was too lengthy to be exposed early. He would have to find something below deck. Maybe a spot among the exports would be more efficacious. It wasn't likely that the crew would rummage through the exports—at least not at the beginning. They'd be too busy running the ship. A hiding spot in the export goods would have to do until he could find something better—or until he figured out how he could better blend in with the crew. Maybe he could study their habits for a few days and slip into the barge's operations without anyone noticing.

The first storeroom he came upon was filled with livestock. It was not the place for him to hide. There was no doubt the crew would be down to tend the animals, and Matthew had no desire to spend hours cooped up with bleating goats and chickens.

He kept looking. He left the livestock deck and found a staircase that led further down the belly of the barge. Crates were stacked high from the deck to the ceiling and were filled with every export Triton could produce. The crates closest to him were filled with gemstones. He assumed they would be sold for jewelry making. Undoubtedly diamonds would be onboard as well, but Matthew knew they wouldn't be kept with the rest of the goods. They'd be in the captain's quarters, locked away.

Matthew moved further down the row of crates, some filled with linens, dyes, or weapons. Other were filled with nonperishable food or medicine. He stopped over a crate of medicine to try to decipher what his father was selling when a shout from behind made him jump.

"Hey!" the crewman shouted.

Matthew tripped over the crate at his feet and knocked into a stack beside him, dumping gunpowder all over himself and onto the surrounding floor. He coughed through the cloud and tried to shake the powder off him. The crewman made his way down the row of crates to stand behind Matthew.

"Well, well," the crewman mocked. "How did you get out here?"

The man grabbed the back of Matthew's shirt and yanked him to his feet. He forcefully pulled Matthew through the door to the stairway and led him by the neck down several flights of stairs. Matthew tried to speak but still fought against the gunpowder in his lungs while furiously trying to clear it from his eyes.

Their collective movement stopped while the crewman unlocked a door in front of them. Matthew was muscled into the newly opened space and stumbled to the ground, helpless against the force with which he'd been pushed. He scrambled to his feet ready to protest the way he'd been handled—ready to defend his position to the captain. Ready to use his royal positioning to bargain his way to their next stop. But before he could speak, the door in front of him slammed shut and the words disappeared in his mouth. The only sound he heard was the lock that sealed the door in front of him. It echoed into the empty air around him with finality.

Matthew yelled and tried to push the door open, but it didn't budge. It didn't even whisper against the full force of his shoulder. He knew his efforts were futile.

He was locked in.

A stirring in the dark behind him sent his nerves to tingle. He spun around, consumed by fear at what he might find as a new inmate. As his eyes adjusted to the blackness, his adrenaline slowed just enough for his senses to begin to turn back on.

First, his nose twitched at the earthy ripeness in the air around him, an undesired blanket of realization. Then his ears tuned in to the breath—the breathing—that filled the cabin in front of him and beside him and all around him. And then so close he could hear the ins and the outs of a heart's production nearly upon him.

His eyes, the last to focus, turned on inside a nightmare. Real, and right in front of him.

Eyes stared back at him.

Recessive eyes.

Hearts beat back at his.

Recessive hearts.

At first, he was afraid, unsure of what they would do to him. He couldn't help but be scarred by his experience on Triton. What would they do to him when they realized who he was? They'd thrown rocks at him while he was protected by the royal guard. What would they do to him when he did not have army to surround him? His mind raced with the possibilities.

But they didn't move on him. Instead, a dirtied hand reached out toward him. In it, was a beaten and worn canteen, filled with water. Matthew lifted a trembling hand to receive it and noticed his own unfamiliar darkness. The gun powder that covered him turned his complexion a dirtied brown.

In here, he wasn't royal. In here, he wasn't pure. He was one of them. He was a tainted Triton stable boy. The crewman hadn't recognized him. Neither did the recessives that surrounded him.

In an illuminating moment of horror, Matthew realized what was happening.

These were humans locked in the belly of a Diamond Isles & Triton barge. It was his father's ship. It was his family's ship. And these people were exports for sale. All of them.

The adventure Matthew had leapt into grew into a monster he could not have imagined. In his wildest ideas of his father, he would have never considered this a possibility.

Matthew worked the situation through his mind again, unable to grasp its realness.

His father was selling humans.

And now... Matthew was one of them.

CHAPTER NINETEEN

ISSACHAR

Agon

The clang of weapon on weapon was a noise so familiar to Issachar that from across the arena he could pick out who struck harder, and with what weapon he struck. Today he stood, as always, watching the highest-ranking Agonian officers sharpen their approaches.

He'd take his turn in a moment. And he would best every one of them. Plumes of dust rose from the dirt and hovered over the pairings as they spared. Strained exertions and forceful clashes filled the air and bounced off the walls of the complex. The men didn't come to compete. They came to learn. The competition ended the day Issachar took the rank as chief, and they all knew it would be decades before that would change.

Issachar watched the men practice, sharing techniques and repeating strikes, advances, and retreats until they were as familiar as walking. This was the heartbeat of Agon. One immoveable army gathered around one cause: protect land

and people. Issachar knew they would remain an authority in Physis as long as they could continue to agree on that.

Issachar observed the men with pride. Having grown up beside many of them, he remembered the days when they would sneak out for a midnight swim simply because it was the most dangerous thing they could imagine. He remembered quarreling over the affection of women and showing off their newest weapons to see whose was the sharpest and the shiniest. And now here they were, grown men, with families to care for and land and homes of their own.

They would spend the first hours of the day training in the arena with Issachar before breakfast. Then later at the dining hall, they would meet the boys and men they trained in their respective areas and begin their long day's work. While they did, several Agonian ships and warriors would fight in the field at the warfront. And every few months, they would send fresh troops to replace them, bringing tired warriors home and sending fresh and rested fighters to the front lines. It was a system that worked well, and it'd worked well for years.

The absolute physical authority in Physis, Issachar was proud of the reputation Agon had sustained. Territories both feared and envied them, and Issachar was determined to lead them in a way that preserved what the generations before him had created.

Other than his girls, there was nothing was more important.

Hours after the leading warriors moved into their respective groups for training, Issachar remained in the arena, refining his own skills. To be chief, he would have to remain the physical champion of the land—it was the law of Agon. Issachar spent every morning and some of his afternoons here, disciplining his body to mastery. He was yet to meet a well-matched opponent, and he did everything he could to keep it that way.

Sweat shot off his body, not in the passivity of a drip, but in a helpless, subservient flight to his command. This was the sole purpose for which he was made. He knew it, and every cell in his body knew it and they sung shared submission to every one of his strikes. He worked his skills over with the men who were deliberately chosen for him to practice against. The men were selected with intent, for the specific purpose of refining Issachar's skills. It was a highly-valued team in Agon—second only to the glory of chiefdom itself. They were, by the very nature of their task, impeccably trained warriors.

Issachar faced each one until his opponent lost his feet. One after the other he grounded a warrior and then made his way to the Chief's Wall, where his weapons hung carefully, having been shined and sharpened for the day's work. He would replace his weapon, choose a new one for a fresh match, and begin again. He handled the weaponry with care, respecting each for its uniqueness, using each for a refined and specific battle tactic. In the strictest of Agon's traditions, no one handled the chief's weapons but himself—not even to clean them. And Issachar honored the ritual by cleaning and hanging each one, every day.

After putting Phineas into the dirt for the third time, Issachar nodded him out and made his way to the wall for a weapon change. Phineas was an able fighter, and one that challenged Issachar more than most. His physical stature was astounding, and it made his agility perplexing and majestic to study and train against. Issachar knew his favoritism toward Phineas was widely known, but it didn't matter. It wasn't Phineas' abilities in the arena that produced the chief's favor toward him. It was his loyalty.

Loyalty was everything in Physis. It was the universal code of honor. Issachar had no doubt that Phineas would die in a moment to protect anyone in Agon, let alone the chief or a member of the chief's family. Phineas, and men like him, were what made Agon great.

Issachar watched Phineas bounce up out of the dirt and push the sweat off his body. He would take a swig of water and be back in line to fight again, cutting the line from those who chose to take longer recoveries. Issachar nodded his approval to Phineas across the arena—much communicated though nothing said aloud. It was respect in its purest form, and a common wordless language among the warriors.

Issachar shook out his limbs while his new opponent approached. Jonas.

Jonas was the last man standing when Issachar won the chief position. Single elimination battles took many warriors' lives in Agon in pursuit of the chieftain status seat. It seemed to Issachar to be a great waste of good men. In his own pursuit, he'd made a goal to eliminate as many warriors as possible without killing them, or even better, without disabling them.

A skilled enough fighter could do it easily.

Jonas had used the opposite approach. He laid bare his insecurities with every swing and killed men who would have been tremendous assets to the Agonian war force. But regardless of his tactics, Jonas too, made it to the last battle for the chieftain seat. And although he lost to Issachar, that achievement made him second in command in any given situation—whether Issachar liked it or not.

"No mercy, Chief," Jonas said as he tapped weapons with Issachar.

Issachar dismissed Jonas' regular greeting with his first offensive swing and the clash of their weapons protested each other and consumed the open air of the arena. It was common during these moments for Jonas to bring up what was on his mind, choosing their physical combat to address the political kind. Issachar wondered if it was simply Jonas' tactic for distraction during their round, maybe a far-off hope to best their leader in front of the others. Or perhaps more likely,

Jonas was simply too much of a coward to raise his opinions to his leader without the diversion of a fight to ease his discomfort.

Issachar knew Jonas' reason didn't matter. A couple advances into the round and Jonas began his exposition as always.

"The warfront," Jonas began.

Issachar did not remove his eyes from the analysis of Jonas' body movements. He only nodded into space to acknowledge his awareness of the topic Jonas mentioned.

"We've not made progress in a year."

"No?" the chief questioned. "We're protected." He spoke between steady breaths. "Our borders are strong." Their weapons met aggressively and then recoiled to strike again. "Our front-line forces are strong." He ducked to miss a swing from Jonas, who'd moved in with an aggressive approach while the chief spoke.

"That may be true," Jonas returned, "but we've eliminated no one in over fifteen months."

Jonas retreated from Issachar's approach and repositioned himself for more. "We swat at our enemies like flies from a cow."

Issachar noticed how Jonas' voice grew with intensity at this point, knowing he'd show a weakness in his momentary passion.

"We allow them to reorganize and attack us at will—ugh!" Jonas took an elbow into the gut cutting off his words. He rolled away from his chief and repositioned himself for another approach. "No elimination means no progress." Jonas slowed now, the last hit holding on to him. "Chief, we ask Agon to give up its men to fight for our power. Shouldn't that sacrifice be for more than the status quo—"

In one motion, Issachar swept Jonas' legs from under him, knocking him onto his back and stealing the air from his lungs.

Issachar stood over Jonas breathing heavily from their

round.

"The status quo looks pretty good to me," he said with his arms raised out to his sides. "Look—people are safe, the crops flourish, we have all we need to thrive." He wiped sweat from his brow, knives still wielded in both hands. "What more do you want, Jonas?"

Jonas stood to face the chief and in between strained breaths, he said, "Physis."

Issachar watched Jonas squint against the pain in his ribcage, but it didn't stop him from continuing.

"I want Physis," Jonas repeated straightening. "Agon deserves it." Jonas looked Issachar dead in the eyes with a directness that made Issachar uneasy. "Why stop at one territory when we can have them all?"

Issachar stared at Jonas, wanting to protest but feeling there was some truth to what he'd said. Agon did thrive. What if *all* Physis could thrive like Agon did? Was he doing his duty by merely protecting what they had? Agon had never played for the offensive before, but that didn't mean they couldn't.

In the chief's silence, Jonas spoke again. "Consider our greatest opponent: he sits on his throne in the Diamond Isles while his men are at war, mining their resources and piling up a fortune, buying himself allies in every corner of Physis. It won't be long until they buy us too—and if they can't, they'll have enough allies among the sea to take us by force."

Issachar walked to the wall to change out his weapon. He carefully hung his knives and picked up a broadsword, shined and ready for his use. He turned and nodded to the line of waiting combatants, signifying his desire for a new opponent.

Jonas may have been able to go another round, but Issachar had heard enough for the day.

CHAPTER TWENTY

MATTHEW

Aftodia Marketplace,
Territory of Kolpisi

Light poured into the cabin and Matthew strained against it. Although he and the other captives had been allowed to see above deck every few days, it was an adjustment getting used to the brightness of light after the unforgiving black of the cabin below.

Today was no different, except for one thing. They weren't moving.

What had become the familiar sway of the ground beneath his feet was absent. Stillness met and unsettled him in a way he didn't know it could. Wherever they'd been headed over the last weeks, they'd arrived.

He squeezed his eyes shut and turned his face away from the sun while submissively allowing his feet go the way they were pushed. The physical discomfort of the trip was something Matthew had never dreamed he would experience in his life, and he was unsure how to manage it. He wondered if the Triton natives lived in fear of the journey he'd just been forced to take. He wondered if they knew the possibility of the nightmare that sat so close to the shore of their home.

Matthew warred against the hunger that cramped inside his stomach every day. He forced himself to breathe when the air was so thick with the stench of bodies that he didn't think he could inhale it one more time. He'd always hated the emptiness of his large and open bedchamber, but with people pushed so close against him he could feel their breath on his skin, he would've given anything to be back there, silence and solitude his most-welcomed companions.

Matthew spent hours at a time trying to talk himself into not screaming into the darkness that surrounded him. He couldn't make sense of his reality. He couldn't make sense of the fact that his father manufactured it. He couldn't help but wonder how many people had been sold, and how his father used the profits of their lives.

Considerations of the fresh and bitter truth of the isles built up under Matthew's chest like a lead-filled balloon. Had his mother known? He couldn't bear the thought of it. He pushed it from his mind and wondered instead where they were. He wondered if somehow, he'd managed to get closer to Zoar.

He knew that discovering what his mother wanted him to know was the only thing that had kept him alive during the past weeks' journey. He had to pursue it. He had to find out why that single word was enough for his mother to hide and hold onto until after she was gone. Its mysterious proffer of life had somehow offered him the resilience to make it this far. He could only hope it would be enough to sustain him through whatever came next.

For now, that one-worded letter was his only lifeline.

Matthew was shoved into a line formed from his fellow captives on the barge. Crewmen divided them by some uncommunicated standard and began to march them forward.

He observed what he could beyond the push and pull of the bodies that surrounded him.

Several foreign ships lined a marina and were marked with the names of territories he'd never heard or seen before. Each vessel buzzed with crew unloading cargo. Teams of men worked up and down the gangways of each ship in undisturbed currents of purposeful movement. Cargo distribution was one-way. It was coming off the ships and onto the land. There were no fishing boats headed out for the early evening catch. There were no cafes on the streets serving travelers. There was no visible housing, temporary or otherwise. There were no natives, no children playing by the shore, no ding-dong of local business. Palm trees hung untrimmed layers of fronds over each other in crowded sections of dead green. They bent with the weight of the excess, curling over brown sand beaches. It was a rocky sand, much like that of the isles, but much dimmer to look upon. It made the island glare with a beaten brown haze that looked dull in comparison to the sparkling white of the rocky diamond sand in the isles.

To Matthew, it seemed there was only one singular purpose to the land on which they'd arrived. And that purpose, was to buy or sell.

There was only one place like this in all Physis, and he'd only ever heard of it, often wondering if it existed only in legend. But now that he was here, after the last hellish weeks on the barge, "legend" was no longer a word he was willing to let live.

It was real. They were in Kolpisi.

It was said that Kolpisi existed somewhere in the far eastern sea and was ruled by only one law: no law at all. Not a soul in Physis could support what was permitted in Kolpisi and still retain its honor. Stories were passed that Kolpisi had separated itself from Physis before Physis ever existed. It acknowledged no law and ran on no rule. It was where one escaped to break away from consequence. It was where one went to defy shame. Kolpisi was known for its ability to help people disappear and to erase the memory of anyone wanting to forget. Disagreements were settled in any way one could imagine and life was discounted in value by the ship full.

Kolpisi's most reputed asset sat just off the coastal docks—the Aftodia Marketplace. Where anything—and anyone—could be traded and sold without limitation. Matthew had been told that in the marketplace anything could be bought or sold without consequence or judgement, and more importantly, with full anonymity. He'd been told it was a place for thieves, liars, and crooks.

It was father who had told him that.

Matthew smirked at the memory, remembering the superiority with which his father had said it—like Kolpisi was filled with the very scum of the earth. The paradox of it felt suffocating to Matthew as he was pushed forward into a line to be bid upon.

It was happening fast, and there was nothing he could do about it.

He stepped up onto a cement block and looked out into a crowd of eyes. He'd never seen so many people who all looked so different. He'd spent his life on the isles with pures just like him: blue eyes, yellow hair, the pale white of endless winter covering their skin.

Before him now were colors he never knew existed on people. It was striking. It was beautiful. He let his eyes run over face after face and stopped on one man's infinitely black eyes. They took him in and swallowed him.

"Ho!" The midnight eyes raised a hand and grunted.

One, and then another, shouted and raised a finger or a hand until it stopped. Matthew was marked on the arm with a black oil paint stripe and shoved into a bamboo cage with others purchased by the same man.

"A collector," Matthew said to the man next to him. He was

remarking on the buyer who'd purchased them both, along with the five others in the cage, but the man didn't respond to Matthew. He just gripped the fence in front of him and watched the podium solemnly.

Matthew noticed the brilliance of the man's green eyes and the light brown hair that sat atop his head. Just a touch of a lighter shade in both features and the man would've existed in the Diamond Isles as a pure instead of in Triton as a tainted. It seemed even more ridiculous to Matthew now, standing next to the man, comparing their features side-by-side.

How long, Matthew wondered, had the sale of human life fueled the Diamond Isles' success? Had his father thought this up in his lifetime, or was it generations-old? He pondered which scenario would be worse if he was ever able to find out.

Matthew felt his desire to survive burn hotter in his belly. There was more to discover than whatever secret was hiding in Zoar. His heart pounded with new purpose but was hindered at his reality. Right now, he was locked in a cage with no way out. It would take more than wondering and wishing to start making things right.

He watched his fellow captive hold fast to the bamboo cage in front of him, acutely focused on the cement block. He noticed how the man's fixed gaze did not release the proceedings for even a moment. Matthew noticed tension freshly overcome the man while a boy was brought to stand on the block.

The boy had a noticeable limp, and he dragged one foot behind him as he walked. When a buyer asked what was wrong with him, the boy simply shrugged his shoulders and said to the crowd, "born with it."

"Heap," said the man running the auction.

The boy was pushed into a herd of others with missing limbs, limps, or mind differences. Matthew watched silent tears fall down the face of the man next to him.

"Is he your son?" Matthew said softly.

The man's eyes remained trained on the boy, but he nodded, working to stifle the noise rising from the guttural places of his soul.

"What's *Heap*?" Matthew asked.

The man finally turned his eyes to meet Matthew's, anger rising over his other emotions. "It's not where we're going," the man said grimly. He dropped his hands from the bamboo and sat down in a corner, letting his head fall to his knees.

"Mate man, why would you ask that?" A teenager near Matthew spoke to him in a loud whisper. He wagged shame through a thick finger. "He just lost his son. Know better."

The kid clicked his tongue correcting Matthew's behavior and moved into the spot where the man had stood moments before to lean against the bars of the cage. He peered through the cracks and began to watch the proceedings on the cement block.

Matthew watched the teenager for a moment and then asked in a low whisper, "do you know what 'Heap' means?"

The teenager sighed his disapproval at Matthew's ignorance and answered, "the Heap takes the trash, mate. It's why they call it the Heap."

Matthew listened intently, fascinated by the knowledge of someone so many years younger than him.

The kid continued, "if you can't sell 'em, send 'em there." He broke off dead shavings of bamboo as he spoke and raked back his dark hair when his fingers grew tired. "Wish we were going there," he concluded. "Sure better than our end, no doubt about that."

Matthew looked at the kid, who so plainly and surely could speak about a world they supposedly shared. Just moments with him had been enough for Matthew to know that they really didn't *share* much at all. The world Matthew knew was nothing like the world the kid knew, and he shuddered to think what other truths may lay there beyond his vision.

"How do I not know about this?" Matthew ventured out

loud to himself. And although he didn't expect a reply, the teenager offered him one.

"Sure, you do. Everybody knows Zoar," he said flatly. The teenager was sitting on the sandy ground now, fiddling with the shells at his feet, his words far more consequential than he would ever know.

"What did you say?" Matthew asked.

Matthew's voice heightened when he said it and it awoke the teenager enough to get his full attention and answer.

"I said, everybody knows Zoar?" The teenager seemed confused at Matthew's excited response to his common words. He continued in Matthew's silence, "Zoar? The Heap is Zoar. Same place, mate."

Matthew turned quickly and strained to see the group considered trash as they were gathered and pushed toward the ship bound for Zoar. One by one they rose higher on the gangway, unchained and unrestrained, into the belly of a large, dark ship.

That's the ship he needed to be on.

Now, all he had to do, was figure out how to get there.

CHAPTER TWENTY-ONE

JONATHAN

Zoar

Jonathan dipped his head and let the cold water from the spigot run over him through his thick, coarse, dreadlocked hair. It made its way through each strand and off their respective ends into streams of clear rope that splashed across the floor at his feet. He remembered dipping his head down the same way, letting the water overcome him while he stood under the falls of the Western Bay.

It nearly four years ago now. And Jude had stood next to him while they laughed at each other under the overwhelming rush of the falls...

FOUR YEARS EARLIER

The water fell a little harder than normal, having just welcomed a sustained rain the day and night before. Jonathan knew Jude was talking to him, but he couldn't hear the words over the rush of the waterfall around his head. He watched it run down through his dreads, across his tattooed arms and legs, and off the rock under his feet to the clear pool below.

He loved this place. He loved coming to climb and jump with Jude. He loved floating in the water below with his ears under water and his eyes above it, muffling the noise, while making more brilliant what his eyes could capture.

Jonathan opened his left eye just far enough to see that Jude was talking to him. The rushing water over and around his ears was too much noise to make any words out, but he could guess what Jude was saying—he'd been talking about this girl for the last hour. Jonathan thought she must really be something. He'd never seen Jude so taken with anyone, or more accurately, with anything—ever.

Jonathan watched Jude wander around, struggling to find purpose and direction over the last few years. And he'd wondered what it would be that might finally capture him— what it might take to get him to commit to something. The one thing he would not have guessed, is that it would be a woman. Jude had never seemed all that interested before, although plenty of women had tried.

Jonathan reached out to knock Jude in the shoulder to get his attention. He yelled over the sound of the water. "Mate! I can't hear a thing you're saying!"

He watched Jude pause, processing what he'd just heard, and then doubled over with laughter. He nodded at the water below, and with silent consent, they plummeted off the rock and into the blue.

PRESENT DAY

Out of the shower, Jonathan was toweled off and donning a fresh set of clothes when he heard a familiar clang from the kitchen. Mae, undoubtedly. She'd been here every day for over a week, forcing him to eat, shower, and clean his mother's house. She refused to let him settle into self-pity. And she'd made it clear she was well-aware of his love for Collette and was simultaneously empathetic and disapproving.

Of course, she knew. She didn't miss anything.

Jonathan didn't mind her knowing. It made him feel a little less lonely to know it wasn't just his secret anymore. Mae's ruthless love reminded him of his mother, and having her there every morning, though intrusive, caused him to feel a little closer to normal. He still wasn't ready to make an appearance up the hill, but he was glad to feel his mood start to shift—like the stone inside him might slowly be giving way, even if ever-so-slightly.

Mae was good like that. She wouldn't quit until he was better, and he knew it. He rounded the corner to the kitchen and stopped dead in his tracks.

"Good morning, doctor," Collette said cheerfully, dipping her head at him.

Jonathan choked on his words, offering only a stare.

"Good morning, doctor," she repeated. He knew she awaited his customary response—one they'd shared for years, since the day they began apprenticing together.

He knew she wouldn't let it go, so he did what he could. "Good morning, doctor," he managed.

"Come. I've made you breakfast." She smiled toward a filled plate on the table.

"You cooked?" he asked carefully as he approached. Collette had a reputation for her skills being more appropriate to the medical table than the kitchen table.

Collette chuckled her reply. "Ladies and gentlemen, he still has a sense of humor. I think he's going to be fine."

She winked at him as she walked and gave an inaudible round of applause in the air. She sat the last of the meal on the table and took the place across from his plate. Jonathan watched her sit and after a moment, forfeited to the scene. It was inevitable. Her iron will was a match for none, let alone a fool who was in love with her. He took his seat across from her, as he had a thousand times before, and warily examined the food before him.

"Is it too soon to tell you how angry I am with you that you have not come to visit us yet?" She said it in her one-of-a-kind way that arrested his defense.

"I'm sorry," he said simply.

He thought about trying to explain. He thought about giving in and ripping through the blockade he'd packed around his heart. He'd considered it more than once in the last few years they'd spent together. But he didn't, and he wouldn't. He couldn't.

"I should've come," he concluded.

Collette tilted her head at him and broke out a smile. "Very well," she said. "You'll come today." Her straightforward tone gave him no room to argue. "My daughter, Josephine, is dying to meet you."

"Josephine," he repeated. It was his mother's second name. It was a name she loved. It was a name that meant 'God will increase.' And Sarah said she hoped He always would.

"We're calling her Josie," Collette said smiling at him.

Collette wouldn't have known, but Jude did. And Jude would have told her what it would mean to him. And Jude would have known it would break down Jonathan's last wall. And it did.

Jonathan dropped his eyes to the plate in front of him and swallowed rising emotion. He let go of an empty fork, straightened, and pushed back his chair. And with a forceful clear of his throat, and a timely, shattered resolve, he said, "well, let's go meet her."

Jonathan pushed cold water past him, breathing once every five strokes. His muscles strained against the speed with which he forced them. Visions of the past day clouded his brain, refusing to leave his consciousness.

The mix of joy and relief on Jude's face was evident from the moment Jonathan stepped through the door. The emotion-filled embrace that followed said everything there was to say. The pride with which his brother presented Jonathan with the flawless baby girl blended to unease at having such a possession placed in his muscled arms. The steady presence of Mae beside him and the affirmation behind her expression leveled Jonathan and kept him balanced when he needed it. The role of 'mother' enveloped Collette in a new skin that looked more natural than anything ever did before it.

Visions of the day scrolled through Jonathan's head, one after the other, filling his mind and then pushing one out for the next. The most dominant scene, however, was one he didn't think he could ever forget. It was what pulled him from his slumber and drove his feet to the water. It was what was fueled every stroke, until it crowded out everything else in his head, heart, and soul.

Contentment was the only name Jonathan knew to call it. It was something that eluded his soul. But his lack of knowing it inside himself did not impair his ability to recognize it on Jude.

Just months before they'd been at the height of weariness—all of them. They were sleep-deprived, stressed, and desperately groping for life both on, and off, the Refuge. Jude above deck and Collette below, Jonathan knew they'd hardly seen each other for weeks and it wore on them both.

Jonathan couldn't help but enjoy the face time with Collette, but he could see the burden of absence on her expression.

That discontent, the strife of the last months on the Refuge—none of it was here. His best friend and the woman he loved were *happy*. They and their child burst with the joy of new life. It so filled the house up the hill that Jonathan wondered how it didn't split it at its very seams.

The ache that dug deep inside him wasn't going anywhere. It found a home. He desperately missed his mother, and he knew the pain would not ease any time soon. And Mae only confirmed it—many times, in her own process of grief. The two people he loved the most in the world were consumed in their love for each other and their new child, as they should be. His last hope for a distraction, the Refuge, and its mission, would be docked as long as Jude wanted it to be. And Jonathan knew if it did disembark again, there's no way Collette would be on it.

At least there was that. At least he wouldn't be delightfully condemned to work side-by-side with the woman he couldn't love.

When his body couldn't pull against the sea any longer, he buttoned on a loose shirt and walked to the café for breakfast. He wouldn't risk another sneak attack from Collette—and he was too hungry to pretend to eat her cooking.

"Good morning, Doctor."

The woman who greeted him had no idea she used a phrase that injured him. He searched his memory for her name but came up empty, so he smiled a greeting instead. After she showed him to a table, he noticed her speak with another waitress before returning.

"What can I get you today?" she asked brightly.

Jonathan gave his order and stared at the water in the glass before him. He tried to push the ache from his belly and the visions from his mind, redirecting his thoughts again and again against his heart's wishes.

The waitress returned and poured water into an already-full cup.

"We're glad to have you back." She shifted often and fiddled with the hem of her shirt while she spoke. "It's very brave what you did—what you all did," she corrected.

He smiled at her weakly and nodded. Silence was the best response he could offer her.

"Well, I'll be back. Let me know if you need anything."

He was relieved when she walked away, but when his thoughts returned, he wasn't sure solitude was the right choice for him either. A young man at a table nearby interrupted Jonathan's thought.

"Wake up man," he said. "She is so into you."

The others sitting with the young man snickered and nodded their agreement. Jonathan squeezed his eyes together still not clear on what they were saying.

"What? Who?" Jonathan asked.

As if on cue, the waitress returned with an unanticipated bowl of fruit, delicately garnished with some sort of herb.

"I know you didn't order it," she said shyly, "but I thought, who doesn't like fruit?"

She adjusted the bowl just slightly on the table in front of him. The watching table of young men stifled laughter and Jonathan finally awoke into consciousness. He smiled his thanks, an apologetic gesture for his oblivious existence, and ate quickly and left while her back was turned serving another table.

"You're a coward," he said to himself, while he walked away.

And that was it.

It wasn't seeing Collette in his kitchen that did it. It wasn't the pride in Jude's eyes. It wasn't Mae's hand on his arm that announced the death of his mother. It was breakfast. It was the realization that a lovely woman had absolutely no effect on him.

He was far past too far gone, and he loved Jude and Collette too much to leave it as it was.

Instead of returning to the hill that held his two homes, he let his legs lead him to the only other place they knew to go— the docks.

One of the departing ships would need a doctor.

It was time to go.

CHAPTER TWENTY-TWO

ISSACHAR

Agon

"It's not fair," Elodie whined.

"Darling, it is the way of Agon." Issachar kissed his daughter on the forehead and handed her dirty dishes from the breakfast table.

"All my friends have maids. You're the chief. We may as well be royal, and we don't have a maid!"

Issachar shot a glance to his wife who shared an eye roll at their daughter's complaint.

Elodie protested, "this is abuse."

"In this house, my love, everyone who eats, cleans," he said with a sympathetic smile.

He hated cleaning too, but this wasn't the time to say so. Elodie grimaced her disgust at the dismissal while Issachar and Amora cleared the table. Eden, the eldest of his daughters, came around the corner dressed for lessons.

"You slept through breakfast again," Issachar said to her disapprovingly.

"Sorry, father," she approached him and placed a light kiss on his cheek. "I'm just tired lately."

"Are you alright?" he asked, holding her shoulders to face him directly.

He looked into her big, dark eyes and wondered how twenty years could disappear so quickly. Eden met his gaze and smiled up at him.

She nodded and brightly answered, "we're off to lessons."

She held her hand out for her younger sister and helped her from the breakfast table.

Issachar admired how Eden had taken to her role as the first born, like it was the unmistakable intent of a greater design. She was a natural caretaker and an effortless leader. Most of all, he marveled at the ease with which she existed in her own skin, completely unaware of the beauty and grace that dressed her.

Issachar kissed each of his girls as they departed, winking at Elodie, and pinching a cheek as she continued her protest. Each daughter would spend her respective day in lessons learning literature and languages, dancing, etiquette, sewing, cooking, and most importantly, of Agon's great history. The men of Agon were born, bred, and raised to fight. Most of them wielded weapons as soon as they could sustain the weight of them. The women of Agon kept life in Agon in motion. They were educated. They were entertainers. They were mothers. They were entrepreneurs and inventors. They were anything and everything they wanted to be—but they were not fighters. It was the way of Agon. And with five daughters to his kinship, it was the way it would continue to be, as long as Issachar held the iron.

A few steps behind the girls, Issachar kissed Amora and pushed his way out the door for the arena. Twenty steps down the corridor he heard Jonas' approach. Issachar prepared himself. It would not mean good news.

"Jonas," Issachar greeted him. "What is it?"

Issachar continued to walk while he spoke, and Jonas turned on his heels to keep pace.

"News from the front, chief."

Issachar waited for more, offering silence until Jonas continued.

"We've suffered losses over the last few weeks."

"Send fresh men."

Issachar tried to keep annoyance out of his tone. It seemed obvious to the chief, and Jonas should have known what to do. It was the standard, even if it was a little ahead of the schedule.

"Yes, of course, Chief, except, we've no reserves to send."

Jonas' words hung in the air and stopped Issachar's march to the arena. He turned to face Jonas directly. An extended silence filled the space before him.

"What?" he asked finally.

For centuries this system worked. For centuries they had more than enough men to fight. The surplus was so great at times men would beg to be rotated in. How was it possible that they did not have enough to send for relief?

"How bad is it at the front?" Issachar asked.

"We don't know," Jonas answered tensely.

The calculating politician of yesterday's practice round was gone. The man in front of Issachar was afraid.

"Are the men gathered?" Issachar asked.

Jonas nodded.

"Let's go," Issachar said.

He walked with more urgency now, unsure of what would come of his first real trial as chief—the first real trial the territory had seen since the beginning. Accusations raced through his mind challenging his security and questioning his ability to lead and protect his people. How had he missed it? How did it happen? Had they become too comfortable? How much of a threat were they facing?

As he entered the arena, silence fell over the high warriors who awaited him.

"Tell me," he commanded.

An hour later, Issachar had heard from each of the high warriors. Each one stood gathered around him and looking to him for an answer. To Issachar, only two things were clear. First, for the first time in Agonian history, they may not have enough fighters to handedly win every battle. And second, no one saw it coming—including Issachar.

The level of danger Agon was in was unclear, but he knew they needed to respond—and quickly. Issachar directed his next question to Caius, who was the high warrior in charge of the men just under deployment age.

"How quickly can the younger men be prepared?"

"Two months, Chief," Caius responded.

Issachar turned to address the whole group.

"They are your focus," he said. "All of you."

As much as he didn't want to send young men to war prematurely, Issachar could not think of another other option.

"Ready them. Now."

Issachar watched the high warriors disperse to their respective groups as his personal training group arrived to put him through his daily training rounds.

"Jonas," Issachar said. "You're up."

Issachar knew Jonas had something to say. He'd seen it bursting behind his eyes throughout the debrief, but he hadn't the courage to share in front of the group, as usual. Issachar knew Jonas would be waiting to present it during their spar, and he didn't have the patience to wait it out today.

They were only moments into their session when Jonas started in.

"Use the women," Jonas said.

It was a subject Jonas had presented several times before.

He thought it would give Agon a definitive edge. If they trained the women to fight, they would nearly double their militia overnight. No one would see it coming and Agon could, once and for all, take all of Physis. It was what Jonas had always wanted. It was what every one of his plans and ploys targeted. Singular power and authority.

The urgency of their situation offered Jonas and his ideas a little more leverage than Issachar liked. With the level of unease he'd just witnessed in his high warriors, Issachar was afraid they may actually consider such a tactic, although just a few hours earlier they all would have called it insanity. Issachar, however, would not be scared into considering it.

"No," Issachar said definitively.

"Will you not even reflect on it?" Jonas asked through heavy breaths.

"No," Issachar answered.

He didn't care if Jonas could see through it. He didn't care if everyone could see through it. He would not send his any one of his five daughters to war. And he would not send Amora.

"Okay," said Jonas with a swing. He advanced with a strong step. "I have another idea."

"Of course, you do," said Issachar.

Issachar fought off each blow Jonas offered. He knew he was weakest when he approached aggressively, always making mistakes in his offensive strikes. Issachar watched for his coming misstep and listened.

"Buy the tainted."

Jonas swung hard and stepped too far. Issachar kicked in the back of his off-balanced knee and Jonas ate the ground before him. Issachar dropped to the floor and placed the sharp end of his sword up against the base of Jonas' neck—a move too threatening to be common in the training arena.

"I will never again host a proposition to buy humans to fight for us."

The dull and dark tone of Issachar's voice gave life to the grotesqueness he felt toward the idea. His stomach jerked in response to the man below him. He'd always known Jonas was a coward, but this revealed it on a new level. Buy men to fight and die for a territory not their own? Nothing could be further from the way of Agon.

Issachar felt Jonas nod below the pressure of his sword, and let him stand.

"We're done for the day," Issachar said to the men standing at the wall.

He watched them look around at each other awkwardly. He'd never cut the day short before and he could see their confusion at his command.

"Go," he affirmed.

Issachar exhaled his frustration and walked to the wall to replace his sword. As he hung it, a misaligned knife caught his eye. He walked over to straighten it and returned it to its rightful position. He polished it out of routine and walked down the line giving each weapon an extra touch of care. When he finished, he stepped back and examined the Chief's Wall, each weapon carefully polished and hung by him alone.

He turned around and closed his eyes, lifting his chin to the ceiling. It would be easy to sink into the self-pity of failure. After nearly one hundred and fifty years of success, the shortage happened on his watch. It would be easy to pin it on one of the high warriors. One of them should have noticed. But he knew that would not help. Excuses and shortcuts were Jonas' rule of play, not his.

Issachar had to face it. For the very first time, Agon was vulnerable. And every one of its citizens with it.

CHAPTER TWENTY-THREE

MATTHEW

Kolpisi

From what Matthew could tell, they'd been riding for almost a week in the back of the rickety wagon that carried him and the others to their new owner.

Owner.

He still couldn't conceive of it. But the eight others who were purchased alongside him seemed unmoved by the concept. That fact alone unsettled him in way that he couldn't explain.

They bounced along the unforgiving terrain, being rebuked when they tried to speak, and allowed to tend to their personal needs only every so often. Matthew was in and out of consciousness, the dark overtaking him more often the further they got from the coastline. He'd never been so far away from the ocean, and the silence of the air was sickening to him.

His mind fought against his circumstances, but his body was a broken shell, defeated long ago in the early days on the barge. He was nothing more than a hump of lifelessness to any half-interested observer.

Many times along the journey he'd considered screaming out his truth, exposing his identity and challenging his captors with the consequences of their actions. The Prince of the Isles could not—would not—be treated this way! Did they not know who his father was?

But of course, they did.

His father was the one who gave the order to sell the people on the barge in the first place. His father was the one who allowed for it—who enabled it. He was the one who made it possible. And he was the one who profited from it. They knew who his father was. Every single one of them knew who his father was.

Matthew remembered the flashes of fire behind the eyes of the Triton natives when they yelled their hatred at him and his father. If they found out who Matthew was, they wouldn't cower and return him to his father in shame. They would kill him.

Matthew stopped trying to keep his consciousness. The darkness was more welcoming. At least in the black he didn't feel the hunger tear at his stomach. He didn't remember his mother's death. He didn't have to consider his father. At least in the black his mind couldn't taunt him with realities he didn't understand; and truths that were too hard to bear.

If consciousness was combat, he would welcome oblivion.

Days later, the wagon stopped.

A mix of dirt and sweat clothed Matthew like it'd been there forever.

When first upon the barge, it was a primary concern to keep his hair under his hat. He welcomed the gunpowder he'd smacked into to darken his skin. But just a few days under deck wiped his worry away. There was more than enough grime to go around, and the subsequent wagon ride only helped thicken the disguise.

It wasn't until he was standing in line, watching buckets of water pass closer to him with every fill, that his concern was alive again. He was too far away from the isles for his acquirer to know him, but his pure features would be unmistakable if he couldn't find a way to hide them. As the buckets drew nearer, carrying with them the weight of his survival, all he could do was hope.

An aloof footman mindlessly went about the task of bathing the captives and ushered them into a line that led to a room at the end of a dank hallway. The woman who came to the door took one at a time, and they didn't return. Matthew wondered what happened inside the room. Perhaps it was better to not know. He tried to turn his mind off to it, knowing there was no way around it. The worry would only make it worse, and he hadn't the energy left to fight it.

The woman returned to call him in upon his turn.

She arrived at the doorway and with the smallest flick of her wrist, waved him in. The room was small and held no more than the table and chair that were in it. They were neatly positioned in front of a single mirror. The woman walked in and went directly to the table. With her back to Matthew, she instructed him.

"Sit down," she said.

Once in the chair, Matthew's shoulders sat high above its back, protruding like they never had before. He examined the stranger who stared back at him in the mirror. His cheeks sunk in where they used to flush with life. He had a straggly yellow beard he didn't know he could grow. That, along with the bruises that decorated his cheeks and the bags that hung under his eyes, created a stranger anyone could mistake a recessive. He marveled at how much had changed in the short month since he'd left the diamond castle.

He closed his eyes and envisioned Faith under the tree, realizing he'd finally found a woman with whom he was willing to match; and then he'd left her. What would she think if she saw the man in the mirror now?

The clank of metal hitting the floor behind him snapped Matthew to attention and he turned in the chair to find the woman, frozen in shock. Horror dressed her face, and her hands shook in the space in front of her. The scissors and comb she'd readied to groom him lay on the ground at her feet.

"Who knows?" she said in a hoarse whisper.

She rushed to the door and wrestled a broom against its handle to secure it.

"Who knows what?" Matthew replied hesitantly.

A look of sternness came over her, like that of a knowing mother getting her child to own up to stealing. She walked over to him and with a quivering hand, she touched the three diamonds embedded into the base of his neck. The universal mark of Diamond Isles royalty, and he'd forgotten it was there to give him away. His eyes fell to the floor in front of him.

"No one," he said quietly.

"Stay here," she said.

She was out the door in a rush. She closed the door firmly behind her, shaking her head and mumbling something to herself under her breath as she went. When she returned, those who had been waiting in line to be groomed after Matthew were dispersed. The woman dug around in the drawers to the table and returned to lather his head with a paste that stunk like sulfur and burned around his eyes. She followed the paste with the scissors and a comb, achieving what she'd originally been tasked to do. When she was finished, she stepped back from him, and a black-haired, blue-eyed skeleton him reflected back at him the hell he'd lived through in the past month.

"You listen to me," she said. "You tell no one."

Her reddened eyes shot him straight.

"A Diamond royal sold to this estate..." She shook her head. "Boy, they *will* kill you."

Matthew looked back at her, feeling the intensity with which she spoke down through his spine.

"Do you understand?!" she raised her voice while still trying to keep it muffled.

Matthew could see her heartbeat thudding in her neck and he knew the truth of what she was saying. It's what had kept him from exposing himself before now.

He nodded.

The woman returned to her table once more and then placed a trembling hand on his shoulder. She brought herself closer to him and spoke shakily.

"Quiet, now," she said.

She straightened and positioned herself with intention behind him. The blade flashed in the mirror momentarily and then sent searing pain across the base of his neck. He pulled against the grip she had on his shoulder, but he was too weak to fight it.

He knew it was the only way. It had to be done.

With as much of a grip he could muster onto the arms of the chair, he girded what he could, and let the woman slice out the last drop of identify he had left.

Matthew scratched at the wound at the back of his neck and wiped sweat from his forehead.

Ezer had done her best to stitch the wound after she cut the diamonds out. She even gave him a story to tell if he was asked about it, but he wasn't. She tied a scarf around his neck and told him to keep it there.

"You'll blend in," she'd said.

She was right. They all wore them while they worked. They collected the sweat that poured off their faces in the sun. And the sun—it never stopped.

Matthew's entire body screamed against his newly appointed work. It'd only been a week but the blisters on his hands and the bruises on his knees didn't care. They laid bare the life of luxury he had known all his life and left him wasted in return. Labor and exertion were foreign to his body, as was the heat that beat down on him. He never thought he'd miss the ceaseless grey chill of the isles, but now there was nothing more he hoped for in a day than a single cloud and a brisk blow of an icy wind off the sea.

Matthew was a paradox next to the others, who seemed to thrive in these conditions, like it was as easy as breathing. It looked natural for them, while he limped with every step. He hated the length of each day, and he dreaded the sweat that would cover his body and the orders that commanded his every moment. He resented that the others bonded over a shared hatred for pures. He resented that his neck itched and that his bones ached. But most of all, he resented that at the end of the day, it was his father who had put him there. It was his father who had put them *all* there. He wondered what he would say if he ever got the chance to look the king in the eyes again.

"Back to work!"

Matthew knew better than to ignore the words of a keeper. He lifted another stone and watched a blister break open against it. Blood and fluid spread across it, painting its surface. He lifted the stone to his shoulder and balanced it there before beginning the march to the wall where it would be added to the estate's perimeter. He wondered how many stones on the wall were painted with other people's blood. He wondered how many of those people had bled on account of his father.

He didn't know how or when, but he knew he would find a way to return home.

It was time for the king of the Diamond Isles to be exposed for what he really was. It was time for him to bleed on someone else's stone.

CHAPTER TWENTY-FOUR

EDEN

Agon

Eden shepherded her sisters from their respective lessons, gathering one after the other. None of them seemed to mind their daily sessions as much as she did.

She wondered if it was simply a product of time. Maybe the mere fact that she'd been doing them longer than her sisters drove her to begrudge the routine of it all. Or maybe she had a lower tolerance for learning these things because she simply had no interest in learning them.

If any woman on Agon had the distaste for their destiny as she did, they certainly didn't share it with her. She'd felt alone for longer than she could capture.

When the mastery of a skill was achieved, the women moved from learning to teaching. This was something Eden knew was inevitable. It happened for every woman around her age. It was natural to advance. But it was also something she'd never wanted. Her peers relished the idea of being promoted to master of a craft, bathing in the superiority and achievement of it. But it held no appeal to her. Destiny or not.

Relieved to be released for the day, Eden gathered her three sisters from their respective lessons and began the walk home. She didn't have to listen to know her sisters would be reviewing the events of the day, sharing the gossip from the others, or recounting the flirtatious moments with the boys in training. Although her ears caught the sound, she didn't hear a thing. Her mind, as it often did, existed elsewhere.

"Hey," she interrupted the others. "I'm going to walk by the shore for a bit. I'll be home to help get dinner ready."

Eden pinched a six-year-old Ember on a rounded cheek before departing. She knew the older two would see Ember home safely. She saw them exchange a look. Eden had made a habit of escaping during their walks home lately. The past few months' detours had resulted in her missing chores more than once. She knew her younger sisters were not pleased by her new routine, but their disapproval wasn't enough to sway her.

"I'll be there," she said emphatically.

"Yeah, whatever," Elena said.

"I promise," Eden added.

"Come on, Ember," Elodie held out her hand and beckoned the child alongside her.

Eden offered Ember a reassuring wink and peeled off in the direction of the sea, leaving her sisters to continue the walk home. Her legs knew the course well, and she didn't waste time in progress to her destination. She felt the nearness of the water through the strengthening of the winds and started her turn to the north. A small cave formation in the rock overhung the water fifty clicks north of the big tree cluster. She targeted it with her eyes and moved faster toward it.

A sound behind her in the full jungle bushes startled her. She turned to confront it but found nothing. She waited, listening carefully for another sound to give away her pursuer, but nothing came. Cautiously, she continued, more attentive this time to what might be behind her. The elevation started to climb, and her breath quickened as she worked her way up the rock formation.

Another rustle occurred, nearer this time, and she crouched to hunker close to the rock underneath her. The sound of the waves to her east blinded her ears while she listened for more. Eden looked to each side, as far out in front and behind as she could see. She stayed low and still for a long moment waiting for her elusive hunter to appear. Her heart raced with the anticipation of what would come, but nothing did. She laid her cheek on the rock and exhaled. Wrong again. Maybe she was imagining it. She stood to reposition the bag on her back.

"Ugh!"

The noise escaped her involuntarily. Pummeled by the force behind her, it threw her to the ground while she and her pursuer went tumbling down the rock and into the sand below.

At first, she fought, trying to gain a stronghold on her attacker, trying to grapple for a way to regain her footing and fight back. But her efforts were to no avail. Her hunter was far more skilled than she, and she knew she was beat.

As body turned over body, sand flew like water from the sky, and she made the only move she knew she could make.

She freed one of her hands from her attacker's hold and let it run across the front of his body up to the base of his neck. Once she had a firm enough hold, she raised her mouth to take his.

"That's not fair," he laughed. "You can't kiss me every time you're losing."

"I can and I will," she said decidedly.

"And what would you do in a real battle? Kiss each of your opponents until he stops fighting you?"

She rolled her eyes and snickered. "Ah, but I'll never be in a real battle, will I?"

"Maybe not, but we prepare you anyway." He smiled, kissed her quickly, and helped her up. "Let's go, princess."

"I hate it when you call me that," she replied.

"I know," he grinned.

The opening of the cave welcomed them, the tide always low this time of day. Amafis visited the wall and picked up a sabre and a gladius, one in each hand.

"Your weapon of choice, my lady?"

Eden looked from one to the other and took the sabre from him.

"Very well," he said.

Eden watched him raise the gladius to tap his weapon against hers. She didn't hide the glimmer in her eyes. She saw Amafis recognize it and raise the slightest smile in response. He was nearing instructor-mode where the banter would be consumed by instruction.

"Let's begin," he said.

Hours later, Eden washed off in the sea before departing for home. She'd kissed him for a long time before leaving, knowing it would be another three days before they could coordinate another meeting. And the long walk home was just what she needed to lower her heart rate and wash the excitement from her eyes.

When she entered, Ember came running over to squeeze her around the knees. Eden kissed baby Elysian, who was busy figuring out how to crawl, and then dutifully wrapped an apron around her waist. Eden glanced at a glowering Elodie and Elena and tipped a smug nod to them.

"Told you," she said.

CHAPTER TWENTY-FIVE

JONATHAN

The Physis Sea,
Onboard the *Esperanza*

Jonathan bent over a soldier's open abdomen and strained for light.

"Hold the light closer!" he barked at the assistant.

She nervously edged closer and turned her face away as she held the lantern closer into the opened soldier. Jonathan couldn't tell if she was more afraid of him or the blood. He wondered over her choice of trade and shook his head in irritation at her. He dug around, trying not to puncture anything else, searching to find the bullet that eluded him.

It felt like an all-too-suitable analogy for his life. Always moving carefully, trying not to puncture anything, grasping for that one thing that evaded him but felt like it would change everything if he could capture it.

The edge of his finger tipped metal inside the man. He left his finger in place while he turned the rest of his hand for a better angle to grip it, and then gently pull it out.

"Finally," he said, exhaling. It tinkered into the bowl he dropped it in. "Sew him up."

He spoke to the assistant in stride while moving on to the next patient in line. There wasn't time to cater to her sensitivities. The Esperanza was far less staffed and far less suited for this type of work than the Refuge.

Of course, he'd been relieved to find a ship to take him so soon, but it didn't feel soon. Years earlier he would have said two days was nothing, quick like the blink of an eye. But the two days he waited for the Esperanza to sail away from Zoar— they felt like an eternity.

The Esperanza was one of many whose mission was inspired by the Refuge. Their crew was made up of soldiers from many territories. Territories they no longer claimed. Whether injured, deserted, or lost, they'd, at one time or another, landed in Zoar and decided to stay. Many of the ships had crewmen. Very few had doctors. And Jonathan was more than happy to oblige.

He knew his disposition had not been winsome, but he couldn't bring himself to care. Bitter felt good. It felt thick— like a wall around him. And he welcomed it, like a warm and heavy blanket in the cold.

He moved from patient to patient quickly, moving on from each as he solved each problem. He spoke rarely and only made eye contact when he had to. It was a transaction, and nothing more.

And most importantly, it was moving him toward numb. And that was the goal from the start.

CHAPTER TWENTY-SIX

FAITH

The Diamond Isles

Faith ran from the stables to her bedroom, doing everything she could to avoid the torrent of questions that stalked her in every corner of her home.

Peace lived in the woods. It swam in the sea. It pooled behind the eyes of the horses she rode and fell in flakes from the sky when it snowed. But it did not exist within the walls of her home.

Her home, for the entirety of her life, was nothing more than a word for a building.

She breathlessly took a seat at the desk in her room, tapping the blank page under her hands and adjusting her posture over it. Several times she'd tried to do this. She tried to know what to say, and how to say it. Did she love him? No. She wondered how one could love another after only meeting twice. But she thought about him often, sometimes for hours at a time, usually under a tree just as they were that day.

She considered the devastating blue of his eyes that

seemed to haunt her. She remembered the strands of yellow hair that fell over his right eye and how he thoughtlessly tossed them back with a flick of his chin.

But more than anything, she remembered the sound of his voice.

It was earnest and genuine. It was sincere. It was sincere in a way that couldn't be faked. After all, she would know. She'd been taught well how to perform.

His voice was the thing that kept her coming back to the blank page before her. She hadn't heard from him. Why should she be the one to reach out? But then, he *did* ask her to write... if she wanted to.

Matthew,

I rode Opie by the water today and remembered the wild you had in your eyes when you leapt from the cliff that day. It seemed like a skin was leaving you, like a reptile shedding its deadness. I saw fear in you; but I also saw freedom.

I wonder what your travels have been like so far. I wonder if you've reached the place you're going. I wonder what you'll find there. Word travels that you've gone, but no one knows where or what to say about it.

I thought you'd want to know the king held a private service for your mother. We were told it was quiet and beautiful, just as she was. Pures were invited to visit her grave a few weeks later. I left her a bundle of the blue flowers that grew under the tree where we sat together. You spoke of her so dearly there. I wondered if the flowers overheard you and thought maybe they could somehow recount your sweet words to her.

I hope so, anyway.

The unrest in Triton grows. A band of recessives tried to swim to the isles in the middle of the night. Many died. I can't understand the foolishness of it. If they're going to start a rebellion, they'll have to be more organized about it. I wonder if they'll make it over the sea. I wonder what they'll do if they make it. I wonder what makes their effort worth the risk.

Some of the royal guard has gone. The patrols thin across the isles. They say the king is unsteady, even violent sometimes. I believe you were right when you said your mother balanced him and kept him reasonable. I grieve for him. What must it be like to lose someone so dear to you? It is the burden of life, yet I wish it for no one.

My parents were as angry as I've seen them at news of your departure. Hodes took me away the weekend after. He manifested some excuse about there being comets in the sky only visible from the north side of the island. Of course, it wasn't true. He may read a lot, but he doesn't know much about the sky. I was thankful anyway. I took Opie. Hodes rode Splendid. We had such a time!

I thought of you often, but every time I wished you near, I thought your adventure far grander.

I anticipate the stories of your discoveries as I anticipate the greatest celebrations of each year, and I beg you do not return, until you've overturned them all.

- Faith

CHAPTER TWENTY-SEVEN

MATTHEW

Kolpisi

"So that's the choice I was given," Leroy said, washing his face. Matthew watched him dry himself and change into his night clothes in a mindless routine, decades old. Several of the other captives in the men's bunker listened in as they prepared for their well-earned sleep alongside him.

"My lungs weren't built for the mines. I'd go into a fit of coughing and wheezing so strong I couldn't stand. They weren't keeping nobody they couldn't get no work from down there."

Leroy took the time to sit down on his sleeping mat before he continued his story. He looped his thick hands together and rested them loosely in the middle of his lap. He leaned back against the wall and let the top of his heavy head rest against it. The white of the hair that grew on his face moved while he spoke.

"I was lucky enough to get a choice—most aren't. My ten-year-old daughter would take my place in the mine, or I would volunteer to be sold for labor somewhere where I can breathe."

Leroy spoke with no emotion left to spare on the subject. It was a story he wore in his very bones.

"Really no choice there," he said plainly.

"Oi then, how long 'av you been here?"

It was Charlie who asked. He was young and inquisitive and hard to keep quelled, but it was hard not to like him. Leroy smiled at the boy weakly, and Matthew watched the old man sort through how to answer him. He imagined Leroy trying to decide whether to give the boy hope, or the truth.

"Been a while," Leroy finally said. "I been here a while."

The men silently dispersed or laid their heads back in the quiet that poured in. Matthew laid back on his sleeping mat and stared at the ceiling above him. How many of the people here had been sold by his father? If Leroy had been here that long, is it possible the isles were selling people before his father took the throne? Was this another tradition his father would refuse to accept responsibility for, conveniently blaming the generations of law and rule before him?

Matthew tried to force his mind onto other things. He pictured his mother at her piano before she'd been confined to her wheelchair. He pictured Faith on the back of her horse, riding obstinately away from him the first time they'd met. He relived what it felt like to jump, unencumbered, to the icy blue depths that tasted like courage and freedom and new life.

"Mr. Leroy?" Charlie's fresh voice ripped Matthew from reminiscence.

"Yeah, boy," Leroy answered.

"Will we ever go home?"

Matthew spotted Leroy's silhouette in the dark. The old man lifted a heavy hand from behind his own head and placed it gently on Charlie's. Matthew could see the shimmer in the old man's eyes and watched his chest rise and fall deeply.

"No, boy," Leroy said.

He patted Charlie's head and then curled inward and turned to face the wall. Maybe he'd thought to give the boy hope, but Matthew was glad he didn't. Hope was fickle at her best and cruel at her worst.

It was time he faced the truth. They weren't going anywhere. Matthew wasn't going anywhere.

ONE YEAR LATER

Matthew slung a bale of hay over each shoulder and strode for the barn.

Months earlier, when he tried it the first time, he had to study the way the other men did it. They lifted the hay onto their shoulders in one swift motion and balanced the bales there as they walked, secure and unmoving. Easy enough.

As it happened, it was much harder than it looked.

Matthew stumbled with every few steps, trying to balance the hay on his shoulders while the bales ceaselessly wobbled and fell to the ground, mocking his efforts with every straw. He dropped the bales, and then dropped them again, and by the time he arrived at the barn, the trail of hay behind him and the shreds remaining in his hands laughed at his efforts—along with the rest of the men. Men, or more accurately, anyone, who felt the freedom to openly mock him was still something he had not grown accustomed to—even after more than a year on the estate.

Today though, Matthew was the one who moved with ease. An observer could have assumed him to have done it all his life. He tossed two bales onto the ground behind the barn and went back for more. Sweat dripped down his back, shoulders, and neck unnoticed. He picked up two more and started the trip back, breathing in rhythm with his steps.

"Good morning, Monroe."

A group of young women approached the barn, led by the young lady of the estate.

"Ladies," Matthew returned.

He dropped the bales and returned for another trip. It'd been a year, but it was still odd to hear people call him by his second name. He'd decided to take every measure possible to secure his anonymity, and although it'd taken a full month before someone cared to ask him for his name... he was ready when they did.

The women giggled as they prepared to ride, shooting blushing glances from each other to him. There was a lot that Matthew had to get used to in Kolpisi, but copious amounts of attention from women was not one of them. He sailed two more bales onto his shoulders and commenced with another trip.

"Hey, Monroe!" Leroy yelled at him from across the field. "They want you at the wall!"

For the past several months, they'd worked on stacking stones high enough to build a wall around the estate. It was hot, the cement was thick, and the stones wobbled in the stillest of winds.

Matthew much preferred work in the barn. He preferred the company of horses over men any day. Especially Pepper. Beautiful and unruly, he couldn't help but be reminded of a wild beauty he used to know when he was around her. He snuck her sweets to ensure her mutual preference for him and spent free moments telling her about his day and a fellow wildling she would undoubtedly admire. Faith shared with him once that Hodes and horses were her best friends. He didn't understand it at the time, but he did now.

There was a lot he understood now that he didn't then. He wished he could tell her.

Matthew stacked the bales on a growing pile amid giggles and glances and made his way to the outer edge of the estate. On his way, he passed milkmaids working the cows in the field. He greeted each as he passed, averting the long and blushing gazes for the gentle smiles of the older women. They would share a soft hello or nod their acknowledgement of him in welcome and unhungry ways.

"Yo, Monroe!"

Men from a passing wagon tipped hats and raised calloused hands in greeting. Matthew tipped his chin in return. The exchanges made him smile. On the royal estate, people would cower in fear of him, or blush and run for cover, or spinelessly agree with whatever he said, even if it was ridiculous. But this was *real*. It was simple. And it was unexpected and without obligation.

As he approached the wall, one of the men greeted him.

"Hey man, we need you."

Matthew paused, realizing what warmed him. For the first time in his life, he was *needed*. For the last year, he'd learned practical skills, he'd developed stamina and grit he didn't know he was capable of, and he'd earned the respect of the men and women he worked beside.

He hadn't said a lot since arriving, but these people didn't require words. They just wanted someone they could rely on. They wanted someone to hold a steady stone while they cemented around it. They needed someone who was willing to sweat beside them. They needed someone who wasn't afraid of discomfort.

These things were nonexistent to life inside the castle.

And although the realization of his evolution brought him a moment of ease, it wasn't the salve he needed. The castle's grip was in full force, still executing full judgement over his every breath. And it kept him from being an authentic part of the community in which he now existed. A foreigner at home, and a foreigner here. The castle was in the way in both places, refusing him kinship regardless of the territory on which he stood.

Every story from fellow captives taught Matthew more

about the reality of the oppression that the isles—that his father—permitted. Whether Triton native or not, the stories each person told made him wrestle with what his birthright represented. His hands may not have been the ones to order it, but it didn't matter. Shame colored his insides. How does one reconcile a mistake of one's forefathers—or one's *actual father*?

Within months, Matthew's distaste for his father, his home, and his birthright had developed into a full-grown fire that burned inside him. The unbearable weight of his invisible crown dug into his temples every time he looked into the eyes of one of his fellow captives.

And the only way he'd found to cope with it, was to work.

The more he punished his body, the more it satiated his shame. His work on the estate was his penance; and he would keep paying it until his body stopped moving.

CHAPTER TWENTY-EIGHT

JUDE

Zoar

Josie squealed, toddling away from a coming wave. Her tight curls sprung above light brown shoulders. She was the perfect mix of her mother and father, blending the beauty of the smooth dark velvet of her father and the delicate lightness her mother offered. Jude and Collette reclined in the sand, shaded by the stretching palms that grew high across Western Bay. The sparkling clear water twinkled at Jude as he watched his delight pitter away from her happy chase. He knew she would grow to love the water as much as he did. She had it in her blood—and in her history.

Collette laced her fingers through his and sighed an agreed satisfaction at the scene. It was something simple and beautiful, and yet the very thing that meant their safety resided only in Zoar.

Josie's too.

Jude hadn't thought about what it would feel like to have a family to protect. He had only ever considered that Collette was a non-negotiable part of his life. He was ready for that. Having a baby girl to protect as well stirred a duty in him that shook him. It was heavy enough to sink him into the very sand upon which he laid.

"So?" Collette asked. "We're agreed?"

She looked at him with raised eyebrows, anticipating his confirmation. After many discussions over the topic, they seemed to have finally reached a consensus.

They would not return to the Refuge.

With each conversation, Jude felt the itch at his feet. It was a feeling all too familiar. It dated back to his school days when he had to fight to keep his mind, and his eyes, inside the walls of the classroom. He felt pulled from books and figures and drawn to the horizon. Its ghostly echo called to him. It beckoned him from his seat to a grander, richer, more adventurous existence.

As a young man, he bounced from trade to trade, unable to commit to one. Mae nagged him. Boredom mocked him. Zoar confined him. He loved the island, but he remembered how choking it felt when it grew smaller and smaller with every sunrise. Not a lot had changed since then—and yet everything had.

He watched Josie's eyes wonder at the world around her. She had it in her too. He knew she did. After a moment, he turned back to his wife, who still expectantly awaited his response.

Collette had changed his whole world. She'd found him in his most restless place, yearning for something beyond what he could grasp or materialize. He remembered sitting here, in almost the exact same spot all those years ago, when they'd had a similarly life-changing conversation...

FOUR YEARS EARLIER

"Jude," Collette said.

She placed a hand on either side of his face and lifted it to meet hers.

"Jude, what do you know is true?" she asked softly.

Her eyes examined him like one of her patients, reaching far beyond the outer layers of him. He exhaled while the wrenching in his stomach worked overtime inside his skin. His breaths were short and shallow and desperate to understand purpose.

"I know there's something in me that is begging me to do something... more."

He spoke quietly, struggling for words to express his internal warfare.

"I know that I love you," he said.

He smiled weakly and turned his mouth into the palm of her hand to kiss it. He closed his eyes, afraid to say out loud the last of his convictions.

"And I know I need to leave."

He'd known it for a long time, but he feared it would mean separation from the one who had captured his soul. And he'd just told her. He opened his eyes to find hers glittering back at him.

"Well then," she smiled. "Where are we going?"

Relief flooded him, and they talked and laughed for a long time while the sun turned the sky orange, and then into a deep and engulfing purple and black. They dreamt out loud about the things they could do together, and about how Jude's bubbling passions could be turned into something productive, something meaningful, even. Something they could live out together. And when they were decided, they walked to Mae's, hand in hand, dreaming of what the next years would be like with the greatest of expectations.

PRESENT DAY

That was the day that changed everything.

It was as if the call that had been forming in him, then beckoning him, and then obsessively haunting him, finally showed itself.

And Collette was the nexus. She'd taken his soul into her hands with the utmost of care; coaxed out a trembling whisper of a dream; and turned it into something real—something that he could hold.

"So?" Collette asked again. "We're agreed?"

"We're agreed," he said.

Looking back and forth between Collette and Josie was all the confirmation he needed.

"I won't put you at risk again," he said. "This is the only place we are all safe."

He remembered the countless times they were boarded. How he agonized over her safety and how she had to pretend to be Jonathan's wife just to survive.

"And I can't leave the both of you here," he said definitively.

In that, there would be no negotiation. He shrugged his shoulders.

"The Refuge mission is being carried on by many others. Mae is concerned we need to pull back anyway."

He couldn't comprehend that they'd somehow started a movement. With so many people being saved, what did it matter if the original ship was still out there?

"I'm glad we did it," he said. "I can't believe we did it."

Josie climbed clumsily into his lap, her hands full of shells she'd found. She squealed at her demonstration, unable to speak with words yet, but still delighted by her discovery. Jude smiled and nodded his affirmation to her, thrilled by everything she did.

"I'm sure there will be times when I get restless," he said.

He noted Collette's wry grin at his comment.

"But this year, just being here on the island with you two... it has been the best year of my life."

He took her and pulled her in close.

"So, if it's okay with you, let's just be here for a while longer," he smiled. "Because this is good."

His kiss had nearly landed when Josie returned with another handful of shells. Laughter fell over them again, and the ease of it felt like all he needed.

Maybe even forever.

The walk home that evening was one of the slowest Jude could remember, and it was delicious. He was surprised by how easy it felt to fill his chest with air. He wasn't aware of the impact the ambiguity of the pending decision was having on him, like a stack of bricks had taken up a home on his sternum without his knowledge of it.

"You seem happy," Collette observed.

He never was able to hide from her.

His cheeks rose. "I am," he said easily.

The decision was made. They would be here. Together. That was a future he could see. It was a future he could look forward to. A small corner of his consciousness wondered if he'd get restless someday down the road, but it didn't feel like a worry for today. It didn't feel like a worry for the next decade. There was too much good in front of him to waste energy on a possibility.

They approached the house on the hill just as dusk fell over the island. Jude's skin tingled at the idea of telling Mae the news. He couldn't wait to see the affirmation in her eyes and feel the assurance in her response. He knew she wondered a lot about what he would do. He knew she was holding her tongue in dutiful support as a loving mother. He knew she would have been amenable regardless of the decision.

But he also knew he was about to grant her the thing for which she'd been longing.

He bounced Josie on his hip as they entered the front door, chanting a nursery rhyme to her utter glee. The door danced on the wooden frame behind them, and Mae appeared from around the corner wearing an expression that was enough to freeze them mid-stride.

"Mama." Jude said it not as a question, but as a statement. One word of knowing and asking, all at once.

"Brother," Jonathan said as he came into view.

"You're back!" Jude exclaimed.

Jude moved to embrace him, but Jonathan gasped and pushed him away. Jude stepped back and watched as his friend came into the light. The bags under his eyes were a deep purple, bringing out the red that lined their lids. His usually muscular frame had shrunk in a way that made his bones protrude in unfamiliar shapes. He wore cuts on one side of his face and had an arm wrapped in a sling that bound it close to his body.

"It's okay," Jonathan said. "I'll heal." He swatted a hand at Collette, urging her away from his injuries.

"I'm fine, that's not why I'm here," he said.

Jude tried to take in the unwelcome sight before him. Jonathan was the strong, unbreakable older brother. He'd only remained on the island for a few weeks before heading back out to service the injured. He was impenetrable. He was a rock of stability. He was stronger than all of them. The fractured frame before him unsettled Jude in a way he couldn't express.

"What is it, Jonathan?" he asked.

"After we were attacked, the Esperanza was ordered back to Zoar." Jonathan said. "All the ships were."

"All of the... but, why?" Jude questioned.

"The council shut us down," Jonathan answered.

Jude's focus shot over to his mother. She was one of the five members of the council. She would not only have known about the decision, but she would also have been one of the five people who'd made it.

"The order says that Zoar will no longer support any rescue aid to the war front."

Jonathan paused before delivering the last of the message directly to Jude.

"The mission's over, brother."

CHAPTER TWENTY-NINE

MAE

The walk over was quiet.

Mae latched her hand just above where Jude's elbow bent inward. He walked with his head down: quiet, pensive. She didn't expect he'd say much. While in this state, Jude's words would be few, and his processing would stay in overdrive. She'd learned that about him when he was a child. She had to let him be. Anything else would lead to irrevocable shut down.

So, Mae chose silence as well, knowing it would give him the best chance to appear level-headed before the rest of the council.

She'd known the order was coming. Hers was one of the only five votes that counted, and it had to be unanimous. She had to vote in the affirmative in order for it to pass. Everyone in Zoar knew that.

Jude knew it too.

The timing of the council's announcement was less than ideal, and it was as much a surprise to Mae than anyone. She wanted to tell him, but she knew he and Collette were getting close to a decision about their own future. And the moment they walked in that night, she knew they had.

And she knew they'd decided to stay.

Jude was a child the last time he looked that free. Knowing that he'd decided to stay was the one thing that gave her hope this morning. Maybe, somehow, he could accept the mission's end.

But deep inside, she knew better. She knew the council's decision would be the fan that relit the flame. And she'd voted it in anyway.

The previous night was a sleepless one for everyone but the baby. The familiar flicker of resolve that sparked behind Jude's eyes was the thing that kept Mae awake. She knew that flicker well. It was his unbending will that set this dream into motion in the first place; it was his stubbornness that kept him pursuing it when all the odds were against him; and it was the unshakeable resolve that set his chin firm when he hugged her goodbye the first time.

They were all back, and they terrified her.

The heavy, old doors creaked their protest when Jude pushed them open. Mae took a deep breath at the site of the gathered council. In their faces she saw a mixture of pride, annoyance, and ambivalence. The conversation was not going to be easy.

Mae squeezed Jude's arm where her hand still held it and left him to take her place behind the table. She nodded her greeting at each of her fellow leaders, unable to lift the sides of her mouth into a smile.

The most senior member of governance began the hearing.

"Jude, before you speak, I'd like to share with you the reasoning behind our decision."

Gregory was one of the first people Mae introduced to Jude after she adopted him. She knew Gregory loved him like a grandchild. She also knew Jude respected Gregory. She hoped it would be enough to keep everyone steady for what was to come.

Gregory continued, "son, the five people at this table are some of the proudest on the island that you began this mission. It was noble. It was a humane aspiration—it exemplifies our island's way of life."

Mae noticed her fellow council members nod affirmation at Gregory's comment.

Gregory continued, "as you know, your mission sparked a number of others to follow in your footsteps. By our count, there are as many as twenty others who have launched out under the Refuge banner since you began."

Gregory shuffled papers under his hands and adjusted himself in his seat.

"Consider, son, that means twenty additional vessels bringing injured soldiers to the island. It means hundreds of additional refugees. It means dwindling medical supplies, housing, food, childcare. The imports we require cost more by the day, and the majority of the people arriving are not only not fit to work but also require intensive medical care in the meantime."

Gregory looked up at Jude empathetically.

"Are you understanding our challenge?" he asked gently.

Gregory spoke low and slow, and Mae was glad. She could see Jude was quelling his anger, trying fiercely to understand even though his every sense of justice fought against the decision they'd made. Silence hung over them like an over-filled balloon seconds from bursting its contents all over the room. Mae achingly watched her son, knowing his insides warred beneath his skin as much as hers did.

She understood the numbers. She knew what the mission was doing to the balance of resources on the island. It was nothing short of devastating; but it was also saving lives. More importantly, the value of life in every form was the belief Zoar held above all else. The conflict of a primary Zoarian belief, and the operational challenge of the mission, was what kept her from voting this in as long as it did.

But then something changed. And as much as she knew it would hurt him, it was time for him to know.

"Raj." Mae spoke to another member of council, seated at the other end of the table.

She made eye contact with him and nodded. Raj and Jude were friends from the start. He was another member of the council who'd known Jude since his first day on the island. When Raj was voted in as the youngest member of council in Zoar's history, Jude led the celebration. Raj was winsome, adept, and level-headed.

He was also the last person, besides Mae, to flip his vote, and he had a good reason.

"Jude," Raj started, "I hope you know how hard this decision was for all of us—it certainly was for me."

Raj cleared his throat uncomfortably.

"You know I lost my Elizabeth a while back." Mae watched Jude nod his response. "What you don't know," Raj said, "is that she died of the fever."

Raj paused and looked down at the table in front of him.

"She got the fever from a soldier she nursed. A soldier who arrived on a Refuge skiff."

Mae watched Jude's eyes work the conflict that arrested him. Raj paused before he concluded, saying the last sentence slowly.

"After that, we lost fifty-seven more."

Mae watched her son drop to one knee when he said it. She'd begged the council to contain the information that Sarah was one of the fifty-seven. She knew none of them wanted to hurt Jude, and it would be too devastating for him to bear. She knew even this amount of the truth would be hard enough. She yearned to rush from her seat to comfort him. She wanted to rub his back and tell him it wasn't his fault. She fought against her maternal instincts to see to her duty. She would have all the time in the world to comfort him.

At least she hoped she would.

Mae glanced down the line of her fellow council members, searching them for mercy. She found no malice there, only sadness.

In the end, that's what changed her mind. All the council wanted was what was best for the island. It wasn't a political choice. It didn't come from feeling threatened or envious or unimportant. It was simply the best decision for the island. A cease-and-desist order on the Refuge mission was the best thing for Zoar. And, if she was being honest, it may also be the best thing for Jude and his young family.

Jude rose abruptly, standing, and facing the table straight-on.

Mae watched a single tear drop from his eye to the floor, carrying with it the weight of fifty-seven heartbeats. Jude spoke then, and it was the blow she feared and yet already saw come. Four words slayed her and were yet four words that made him so truly who he was.

His voice was steady and level.

"I have an idea."

CHAPTER THIRTY

COLLETTE

Collette paced back and forth across Mae's porch while Josie played at her feet. Josie and Chef Jackson were hard at work stacking blocks into towers and doubling over with laughter when they fell.

Collette was thankful for the distraction, and for the company of the ever-jubilant Jackson. Physis could label him a mutant all they needed, but Collette was sure he had a better grasp on life than anyone else she knew. His undisturbed joy proved that over and over during their time on the Refuge, just as it did now.

"Collette is walking and going nowhere, walking and going nowhere..." Jackson sang his observation from the floor. He lifted a block for the tower and moved it back and forth in a meandering motion, and then to an abrupt stop and reversal.

"Go, go, go. Stop. Turn around. Go, go, go. Stop. Turn around," he chanted.

He gently placed his block on the tower and warned Josie

of the impending crash.

"Last one, JoJo!" he exclaimed.

The tower crashed and the pair turned over cackling. Collette gave in to the ease of the moment and watched Jackson excitedly begin gathering blocks back together.

"Should we do it again?" he asked the child happily.

The toddler nodded emphatically, understanding his question though she didn't have the words yet to reply. Noise from the front room pulled Collette's attention away.

Jackson waved her on. "Quit standing there and go find out what happened."

Relieved and thankful for her friend, Collette rushed around the corner and bumped into Mae, who was alone.

"He went to get Jonathan," Mae answered the unasked question. "He wants to tell you together."

"Tell us what?" Collette asked.

She hoped Mae would let on even just a little, but Mae walked right past her, put a quick rub to Collette's upper arm, and went out to greet the tower gang.

"Hello my loves!" Mae greeted warmly.

Collette could hear the celebration from inside the house. She watched Josie abandon the tower to run to her grandmother who swooped her up in a loving embrace.

Collette reflected on how glad she was that they returned to Zoar. She thought about how valuable it was that they'd stayed for the last year. She remembered the relief she felt that she and Jude decided not to return to the mission.

How could twelve hours ago feel like such a distant memory? That lovely evening in the Western Bay together, wrapped in such ease and contentment... how could it all change so quickly?

Collette relentlessly questioned Mae about what happened at council, but Mae gave away nothing, as usual. If it wasn't hers to share, she wasn't going to, and Collette knew her well enough to know to give up the hunt and wait.

The minutes it took for Jude to return with Jonathan were the longest she'd lived in a while. She sat in the front room waiting, trying to quiet the thud from her heels on the wooden floor.

A crash of blocks from the porch made Collette jump to attention, and when she turned back, Jude and Jonathan were arriving through the front door. Finally.

Collette recognized the look that twitched in her husband's eyes. She knew it like she knew her own reflection.

Whether she and Josie were coming or not—Jude was headed back to the Refuge.

CHAPTER THIRTY-ONE

MATTHEW

Kolpisi

Matthew stacked stones on the fence with the others. He wiped sweat from his neck with the scarf that remained there since the day Ezer gave it to him. He knelt onto one knee to toss back a gulp of fresh water and looked around at what they'd accomplished.

They'd made measurable progress, but the project would require years more to complete.

Matthew thought about the fact that he *wanted* to see the wall finished. Something about working toward a common goal with the captives, sweating next to them, struggling with them, resting, and eating by their sides. It was satisfying. It was fulfilling.

Matthew looked forward to each morning. Meeting his sleeping mat each evening was gratifying. It was as if for the first time in his life, he was properly earning the right to sleep at night. He looked forward to the ache of his muscles. He welcomed the drop of his body onto the old, tattered sleeping mat. Even more odd was the desire to greet the captives every day, and the longing to be assigned to work next to some of them. Matthew anticipated their company. He welcomed their embraces. And he was filled by their mutual affection and attention.

Matthew wondered about the foreign feelings that hovered over him. Were these people his friends? He hadn't the prior experience to know it if they were.

He felt warm and it turned the corners of his mouth upward. He looked forward to seeing Charlie's sleepy eyes at the breakfast table. He looked for opportunities to work beside Leroy and hear the stories of a life lived much fuller than his own. He dined with Ezer at every opportunity, learning more of what life in the Territory of Racham was like before she was sold to Kolpisi.

Matthew was greeted from across the estate with ease, a fine juxtaposition to the fear and flattery common to his life in the isles.

These people were not his friends. They were his family. He wanted to finish the fence with them because they did it together. He wanted to shake their hands at its completion. He wanted to stand back and look at something he'd helped build and know he had a crucial part in it—even if it was forced labor.

Matthew took a few steps back from the wall to take it in. He ran his scarf across his face and the base of his neck, moving it smoothly over the well-formed scar where the royal diamonds used to be.

The scar felt far more natural to him than the diamonds ever did, like the scar was the more appropriate mark of his royalty all along. The gratitude he felt for Ezer's swift actions at their removal was more than he could grasp. She continually maintained his revealing features to carry on his disguise. Without her, he was certain he would have been found out and eliminated long ago.

"Heads up!" Charlie yelled from across the field as a ball came flying at Matthew's face. Matthew kicked it back toward where Charlie played with the son of the estate owner. For the past few months, this had become a ritual for the pair. Around the same age, Charlie and Sebastian got along with ease, too young to understand or acknowledge the barriers that would move them apart as they grew.

"Sebastian!"

The woman of the estate yelled at the boy from the main house. The boy kicked the ball back to Charlie and waved goodbye. He would go in for a while, and later, when he could sneak away, he would be out to play with Charlie again.

It'd become the game they all watched at the wall, each captive enjoying the comradery the boys shared. Whether kicking a ball, climbing a tree along the edge of the estate, or hunting mice in the stables, Charlie and Sebastian didn't have to work to be friends.

There were parts of their friendship that made Matthew jealous. He always wished for a friend—or a sibling—anyone with whom he could pass the time. But he had neither. Watching the boys made him pause with simultaneous ease and envy, one sentiment never quite winning out over the other.

Matthew and the others worked through the boys' show, laughing while listening to their juvenile conversations, and chuckling when one would get sore over losing a game they'd invented. The boys seemed to like their audience and made sure to play close enough to have a crowd. The captives welcomed the chance to let Charlie be a kid and they found ways to hide his leisure time from the keepers as often as possible.

Sebastian and Charlie's adventures lasted a full three months when Sebastian stopped coming.

Matthew, along with Charlie and the others, watched the estate house every morning, fully expecting Sebastian to return with an ornery smile and his endless energy—but he didn't. And he didn't the next day, or the day after that.

On the fifth day of Sebastian's absence, Matthew could tell it was starting to get to Charlie. While walking to the estate after the day's work, Matthew placed a hand on Charlie's sweating head.

"I was wondering if you'd kick the ball around with me a little tomorrow," Matthew said to Charlie. "I bet we could find some time while the keepers are away."

The boy's large dark eyes met Matthew's with excitement, and he nodded his consent.

"Good," Matthew returned.

He placed his arm around the boy's shoulders and walked with him to the dining common. The affection Matthew felt for Charlie spread through him. He wanted the boy to be safe and well, and he felt an undue responsibility to help ensure his happiness. Matthew felt more loyalty toward Charlie in the short year and half that he'd known him, than anyone in the rest of his life—apart from his mother.

Matthew marveled at the idea that he would willingly suffer for Charlie if he had to, and that understanding was the first domino for the rest.

This was his home. These people, his community. This is what it meant to *belong*.

His bitterness was gone. It must have evaporated so slowly that he didn't notice its absence once it was gone. He wasn't sure when it finally dissipated its last, and he didn't care. All Matthew could deduce was that with every smile and greeting, his fellow captives had slowly worked the stone inside him to clay. He tried to find the old familiar hate for his father, but the royal life he'd left felt too far away to have any power left over him.

Maybe his penance was paid. Maybe he could turn off whatever was left of the past and forget it ever existed. This was his life now. This was his work. These were his people now. And it all meant something to him.

When they reached the dining hall, Ezer raised a hand and waved Matthew and Charlie in her direction.

"Come on," she said plainly, "better you than any else."

She smiled at them with ornery intent.

"Do you know how many people I've turned away? An empty seat next to me is a prize, so get over here before I change my mind," Ezer said teasingly.

She tapped the bench next to her. It was more a directive than a request, and Matthew rolled around in it.

"Is there room for me, too?" Charlie asked.

Matthew smiled and answered, "definitely."

CHAPTER THIRTY-TWO

FAITH

The Diamond Isles

Matthew,

It may be unbecoming to write you again in lieu of your absent response, but you've learned by now I'm not always becoming.

I find myself riding Opie by the royal estate more and more often. The guard has thinned to nearly nothing, allowing me to get close to where we rode that day, to catch just a glimpse of our memory. The more I go, the more I want to go—whether in hopes of your return or the thrill of riding on royal grounds, I don't know. But I return, at least a few times each week, and ride under high cliffs while searching for your elusive stature. Also unbecoming, I know.

After a time, my parents' relentless curiosity and scornful disappointment lowered to a hum. Now, they hardly look at me most days, as if my value to them has all but vanished with you. Without the ability to leverage me for royal gain, what worth do I hold for them? Indeed, what is the point in my marrying at all if not to a prince? I embellish, of course.

Relief is too small a word. Your leaving was liberation. For us both, I believe.

Triton still threatens mutiny. If I'm being honest, that is the other motivation for my writing you. Unease grows all around us, and the very act of informing you somehow makes me feel safer. Rogue bands of recessives have made landfall many times in the isles. They haven't become violent, but every time they leave a declaration (or warning sign, it's hard to tell the difference) of how far they advanced. Each time their mark is closer and closer to the royal estate.

The last declaration wasn't far from that of my own estate. It was a big, wooden square with black letters painted on it. It read, just as the rest, "Triton." An assertion of their growing strength. And a warning, it seems.

Hodes didn't let me out of his sight for a week after that, and I must say, I was glad for it.

Although I hesitate to continue, you should know there are very few staff left in the castle. Word travels that many have resigned their posts under your father's obstinacy. It seems the loss of the queen has sharply declined his reasonability. The stories are not pleasant, and I will forego details considering your possible sensitivities to them.

I share this because I think it's important you understand—if the recessives make it to the royal estate, your father does not have the protection he will need to survive. It's said that a cook and an elderly housemaid remain. I'm not sure how the two of them will fare against a band of Triton rebels.

I do worry about him, Matthew. He is not a kind man, but he is still the king. More than that, he is still your father.

Apart from my worry, and it can be great, my head is filled with the dreams and vaguest imaginings of what you must be experiencing. How does one dream of places yet unmet by his or her own eye? I have only my imagination to create your travels now, but I hope to receive your stories in the greatest of detail upon your return.

I often wonder where you are, what wonderful and interesting people you may have met, and what brilliant new places you may have explored. To imagine, each turn a fresh discovery! How thrilling and mysterious it all must be!

I hope by now you've found what your mother intended for you. Its mystery stalks me from time to time and I find I must tame my own tumultuous curiosities to keep it from consuming my mind. I must reign it in like Opie on an open plain, wild and unruly until harnessed.

I wonder—if your mother's mystery piques at my interest as it does, how must it taunt you if you have yet to find it?

It's hard to count down days to your return when one is not offered an end to which she waits. But as much as I can, I do.

Find what it is you're searching for, dear Matthew, and then return to me. And as much for me, for the isles.

I believe you will be needed: and soon.

- Faith

CHAPTER THIRTY-THREE

ISSACHAR

Agon

Issachar took his place at the head of the table and waited for each of his girls to take their respective seats. Baby Elysian, nearing her third year, was pleased to be seated with the rest of them. Issachar dabbed at her chin and winked.

The chatter from the girls was the background noise to his life at home, and it played behind his ears as they drew to the table. As was his ritual, he took time to consider the beauty of each as they took their places—each daughter distinct from the others, and yet miraculously the same. Each one an intriguing mixture of he and Amora.

Eden was graced with calm strength. Elena settled herself into a thoughtful and intellectual nature. Elodie danced with a boisterous, funny, and yet willful, combative demeanor. Ember had a sweet and loving countenance. She was ceaselessly curious and equally encouraging. And then there was Elysian, who seemed she may end up a mixture of them all.

Issachar counted the blessing of each child, overwhelmed by how much he cared for what filled their table. He locked eyes with Amora from across the table. She knowingly lifted one side of her mouth up into a wry smile. He knew that she knew what he was thinking. She always could see through him. She was the one person, he thought, who knew how deeply he cared for his girls. She knew he loved them fiercely. She knew what he would sacrifice to protect them. She was also the only person who knew how vulnerable his love made him.

Amora had been a part of his life for so long, he didn't know if he could exist without her, and he prayed he'd never find out. She commonly warned him against the strength of his passion.

"The gift of the warrior is his curse," she'd say, teasingly.

Every time she knew he was falling more in love with her and her girls, she'd remind him it made him all the more vulnerable. Passion was passion, and it made him strong on the battlefield and weak at home. Although it was a common jest between them, it held within it a truth that worried him.

The gift of the warrior *was* his curse, and Agon's new vulnerability made him viscerally aware of it.

The family joined hands around the table so Issachar could lead them in a prayer of thanks for their meal—a tradition Agon carried from its inception. When he finished, the girls started in with their daily chatter, each sharing the gossip and reviewing the events of the day. It was a language he learned while being a father of girls. It took some time, but he picked it up along the way, and he was quietly proud of his fluency. He listened intently to Elodie's dramatic reenactment of the day until the high, shrill blows of alarm sounded throughout the barracks.

Issachar moved quickly, standing, and ordering the girls to the safe bunker built inside their quarters. He caught a questioning look from Amora, who said nothing, but looked confused at his reaction. He nodded to her an affirmation that was enough for her to echo his command to the girls.

"Father!" Elodie barked. "You never make us bunker at the alarms, why are we doing this?"

She was right. The alarm sounded often. Anytime a foreign ship dotted the horizon, anytime a disturbance occurred at their gates, anytime a household door was found out of place, the shrill scream of the alarms covered the skies. Whether in his pride, or his laziness, or his foolishness: he'd taught them not to respect it.

He regretted that now. Especially now.

"Do as I say," he said, corralling them to submission inside massive arms.

"Is something wrong, father?" Eden asked.

He saw the look in her eyes. He heard the lift in her voice.

It was familiar to him, like part of his soul existed inside hers. It wasn't fear. It wasn't trembling. It was excitement. It was the spirit of the warrior, lit by the thrill of conflict, and it stared from her, to him, like a mirror.

"No," he answered.

His voice fell to a deeper low, a new fear engrossing him. He cleared his throat and straightened himself.

"Nothing's wrong. Stay bunkered until the relief sound."

Issachar looked at Amora for confirmation that she would keep them hidden until then. When she nodded, he left for the tower, but not before first visiting the arena for a broadsword.

The relief bell sounded before Issachar arrived at the tower.

The coming ship that set off the alarm retreated into the direction it came. That was what Agon was used to. It's what Issachar was used to.

Whether ignorant vessels retreated upon their realization of their whereabouts, or whether once-courageous efforts turned cowardly at the sight of the "untouchable land of Agon," virtually all foreign approaches turned on their ends to return the way they came.

Many alarms sounded over the skies of Agon, and Issachar watched its citizens, his people, and more disturbingly, his own family, ignore it. Why hadn't he noticed? Over the strenuous efforts of generations past, Agon had grown acclimatized to its own sure defense.

Forget the warrior shortage, this faux comfort made Agon more vulnerable than anything else ever could. They felt safe. And they were not.

The territory needed retraining, but how could he do that without creating fear in the people? How much should be shared about their vulnerability? Would the people side with Jonas and call for the women to fight? That idea was a freshly pungent hell having just seen a thirst for war inside his eldest daughter's eyes.

The young men they readied to meet the shortage were younger than Issachar was comfortable with sending, but they would be deployed soon despite of it. He worried about conditions on the front line and how the young men would fare. The men on the front had been there for a long stint. Their supplies waned. Their bodies would be tired, and Issachar knew higher-than-normal casualties would occur—especially with inexperienced warriors entering the field to replace them. He worried about morale, and about what kind of stories the men would bring home with them to spill across their land. His concerns piled high—higher than ever in his tenure as chief. Maybe even in his life.

Issachar struggled to elude Amora when he returned to the barracks. She knew him too well to let it go, and in the end, it was a relief to let her in. He could see concern in her expression, but she received the news stoically, as was her way. She was a rock of a steadfast nature, and the simple act of saying everything out loud comforted him more than any strategizing session could.

Amora was as opposed to the idea of training women to fight as Issachar was, and just as disgusted by Jonas' suggestion to purchase humans to fight their war. She concluded the same way the high warriors did—speed up the younger men's training and deploy them sooner. She also offered her support in retraining the citizens to respond aptly when the alarms sounded. That training would start with the girls under their own roof.

"We need humility," Amora said, simply.

It was pointed, and it was true. And it was a challenge Issachar never saw coming.

Before they dispersed from the conversation, Issachar decided to share with Amora the last and largest concern haunting him. It weighed on him more than the rest, and he was struggling to stand and look it in the face. He knew telling Amora would mean that he would no longer be permitted to ignore it. Exposing his fear to his wife would demand his action and it scared him more than any of the rest of it.

But it had to be addressed. And fast.

Issachar stood in the midnight, hardly able to see a full two feet in front of him. He steadied his breathing, just as before battle.

This would be unlike any battle he'd fought before, but he was ready. Resolve pumped through his veins and fastened him to his position.

He decided against bringing a weapon, and he was glad for it now. The feeling inside him was so similar to the one right before war, he feared the results if he did have a weapon to wield.

He closed his eyes and opened them. Hardly a difference at all. The sound of the rolling tide was rhythmic and loud, and it kept his ears from hearing the approach of his unknowing guest.

The strike of flint on the wall alerted him the battle was near. The torch, carefully held, lit the cave wall where he watched his own chiefly weapons tenderly stacked next to each other, readied for use, as they would be for him the following morning.

He was silent for a moment, watching the routine, far more familiar than he expected it to be.

"Eden," he said softly.

She reacted quickly, dropping the torch, and readying a blade for a fight. She did it with an ease that made Issachar both proud and knotted, all at once. He stepped closer into the light of the torch and saw an uncommon mixture of relief and terror take her. He waited for her to say something, but she didn't. She just stood, frozen.

After a moment of silence, Issachar delivered the one message he'd come to say.

"This ends," he said. "Now."

He placed a light kiss on his child's forehead and walked to the opening of the cave. He thought a few times about refraining from sharing the rest of his news, but he loved her too much to let her be surprised two times in one night.

"Amafis will not be joining you," he said.

He saw the acknowledgement of his knowledge flash over her eyes.

"He was deployed out on the midnight vessel."

The blade she held in her hand fell to the sand, and Issachar turned to leave, his heart breaking, right beside hers.

CHAPTER THIRTY-FOUR

JUDE

Zoar

Jude stood ankle deep in the waters of Western Bay. He lifted crates filled with medical supplies onto the skiff in front of him, while warm, clear water sloshed easily at his feet.

It seemed so long ago, and yet as if it were just yesterday, that he did this the first time. He remembered the way his heart beat heavy and the way his stomach fluttered with the anxious thrill of what was in front of them. Everything was new then—everything yet to be discovered.

Today he filled the skiff knowing exactly what awaited him, devastating and beautiful all at once.

Two weeks had passed since the meeting with council. Twice, he asked Mae if he was doing the right thing, his mind remaining unsettled at his own proposal. Twice, Mae looped her hand into his arm and said what she'd said so many times in his lifetime: "the most valuable humans on Earth, Jude, are the ones who have beating hearts inside their chests."

She answered without answering, but he knew. It was the

code by which she lived. It embodied everything Zoar valued. Her chosen response to his question was what he needed to know he had her support.

There were too many beating hearts to keep beating, and the Refuge mission was how that could be accomplished. He would do it just long enough to keep the mission going—just long enough to convince the council that someone else could take over as its leader.

The agreement was simple: the mission would continue, but under the condition that all relief efforts stayed on the water. No ships would be permitted to carry patients or refugees back to Zoar under any circumstances. Supplies and space on the island was limited and had to be reserved for its own citizens. The agreement would make life on the water more complicated. It would require Refuge ships to deliver recovered patients to their respective territories or fleets—if they could approach without being attacked.

Jude remembered the negotiation with the council. He remembered how sure he had felt that it would be enough of a compromise. He was sure the council would agree. He was sure he could walk away knowing he had saved the mission, and that every ship would be allowed to return to the water.

And the council did agree. They nodded their heads and smiled with pride at his ceaseless adaptability. But they didn't sign off until one final stipulation was met.

For the council's sake, agreeing to the condition took a simple nod of consent from Jude.

Telling Collette would be an entirely different story.

TWO WEEKS EARLIER

Jude absorbed the looks on all three of the faces that stared back at him after delivering the news.

Mae sat in the middle, proud and stoic. She felt every emotion known to man, but she expressed them with the greatest restraint, calculating the effects they would have on the people who depended on her. She sat with her hands folded neatly in her lap, breathing as steadily as ever, a nod of approval at his words.

Jonathan's weary eyes lifted no more than a half-moon open, the purple under them only slightly faded since the previous day. His arm was still wrapped in a sling, and his shoulders slumped like a man twenty years his senior. At Jude's announcement, Jonathan closed his eyes and let his chin fall to his chest. He didn't speak. He only rose after Jude's speech and carried himself down the hill. It was a full week later that he returned through Mae's screen door and asked when they were leaving. Life did not exist inside Jonathan's empty frame, but Jude thought it a good sign that he intended to rejoin them on the water.

Jude delayed turning to face Collette, fearing her response more than the rest. They'd just decided to stay. They'd just decided to give up their life on the mission. The joy that floated him back from the Western Bay only hours before felt like a distant dream, only ever imagined. He waited to look at her, his heart staying his gaze on Mae and Jonathan far longer than could be helped.

When he finally pulled together enough courage to face Collette directly, he knew what he feared the most had happened. She felt betrayed.

A wave of regret rushed him. He shouldn't have agreed to it without talking to her. He should have told the council to ponder it a while, talk it over, think about other solutions. He should have offered someone else to lead the fleet. He should have brought Collette with him to the meeting to prevent him from doing something like this.

But none of that would help him now. He'd agreed to it already. And the council was firm in their decision. Rescue efforts would continue, but Jude would be required to lead them. They would need to be organized, run on process, follow the newly established standard of procedures, and the ships would all have to agree to follow Jude's command. Jude was a non-negotiable part of the deal. The council trusted him. He was a born leader. More than that, he was Mae's child. His inherent desire to honor her and protect her position in the council would be the added collateral they needed to keep Jude compliant.

It made sense. It was a smart solution.

And it was the one thing that was going to turn his world on its end. Again.

After holding Jude's gaze for an extended moment, Collette had stood from her position next to Mae and left out the front door.

PRESENT DAY

Jude stopped loading crates into the skiff long enough to stretch his arms and back. Sweat glistened off his dark skin and ran off him like rain down a palm frond. He pushed it away thoughtlessly and turned to look at the horizon behind him. Not even five years ago, he'd stood in this same spot, looking back at the Refuge wondering what they would discover and how many lives they could save.

Now, there were seven ships on the horizon. Seven crews. Seven times the resources to save lives. Seven times the peace they could provide in a land that had only ever known war. If there were this many people willing to move toward peace and perseverance, he wondered how many more existed in Physis. They couldn't be alone.

Jude wondered if the crews would listen to him or follow his orders. He wondered if they would be as successful as a unit as the Refuge had been alone. He wondered how long it would take to convince the council that someone else could lead the efforts.

"Excuse me, Captain, who permitted you a break?"

Collette lightly smacked his leg when she walked by, recounting what he'd loaded and marking it off on the inventory list she held. Jude scooped Josie up into his arms, who had just begun a new habit of following her mother around like a duckling.

It'd taken the better part of a day, but after an apology and a conversation, Collette came around to the agreement with the council. And not surprisingly, she would not be left behind.

The decision was millions of miles harder this time, because of Josie. Collette was just as passionate about the mission as Jude was. She felt just as strongly about the value of human life, and she believed, even more than he did, that non-violence could win—that peace wasn't just the naïve hope of a dreamer, but that it could be achieved in Physis. The Refuge mission was as much hers than anyone's, and she made it clear that her presence onboard was non-negotiable.

"On land, even captains are allowed breaks," Jude said, kissing the baby. "Josie, how will I keep existing without you?"

Jude kissed her and hugged her until she protested herself out of his arms and back to her own explorations. The impending pain of departure taunted him, driving him back to the tasks awaiting him. If he paused for too long, the fleet of ships floating behind him would not be departing in the morning. They would not be departing at all.

"I don't know if I can do it," Jude said.

"I can't think about it either," Collette agreed. "But what do you know is true?"

It was the question she always had ready when he couldn't move forward. She had asked him the same question the day they sat in the Western Bay dreaming up this mission the first time. And it's what she'd asked him the day he agreed to this.

"I know that this is just temporary," he said. "We go out, we show them it can work, we work out the missteps, and then we come home." He dropped a crate to grab her instead. "For good."

"Yeah," she said dreamily, "home for good."

"I know that Josie will be happy and safe, and be well with Mae."

"Yes, she will," Collette nodded as tears started down her face.

"Okay, you were helping me be brave," Jude said. "If you go down, this whole ship goes under." He wiped the tears from her face and added quietly, "pun intended."

They quietly chuckled together, and he pulled her close.

"It's temporary," he said. "It'll be quick."

He tried to convince himself as much as he tried to convince her. He felt her nod against his chest and sniffle quietly.

"It'll be quick," she repeated.

CHAPTER THIRTY-FIVE

MATTHEW

Kolpisi

The sun broke through the window next to Matthew and he stretched his bones awake. When he'd first arrived in Kolpisi over a year and a half ago, he would wake every morning having sweat through his sheets. In Kolpisi one wore the air most days, the humidity soaking through every layer of skin and clothing. Now, it felt more like a blanket than it did an oppression.

All his existence felt that way.

He smiled at the beauty outside his window and jumped down from his bed. He shook Charlie awake.

"Get up buddy," he said. "Don't want to miss breakfast again."

Charlie moaned and rolled over, nothing new. Matthew would put bread in his pocket for the boy just in case. Matthew loved Charlie. He didn't know if it was like an older brother loves his sibling, or how a father loves his child, but he adored the kid. Being around Charlie, Matthew got the chance to see the world through a child's eyes—something he was not afforded as a royal prince. Now, almost thirty years later, he was discovering the way a child thought about things, the questions he asked, and the possibility found in even the most mundane of settings.

He glanced back at Charlie's bed and chuckled at the boy back asleep. Charlie would most definitely be complaining of an empty stomach in a few hours and Matthew would be ready.

"Morning," Matthew whispered as he passed Leroy.

The old man sat upright on his sleeping mat, engaging in a morning stretching ritual. Matthew remained astounded at how able the old man was. He wanted to grow old like Leroy. More than the old man's flexibility, he had a stillness about him that Matthew searched for long before he knew he was looking for something. He remembered staring into his own reflection in the castle, searching for anything that could move him. Anything that could spark life inside him. Anything that could make him want to wake up the next day.

Looking into Leroy's eyes, it was clear the old man understood something that few others did. The hope of understanding that secret someday felt a little more attainable when Leroy was nearby. He tried not to pelt the old man with questions, but he was desperate to grasp a little more of the peace that pooled there. As long as Leroy would offer it, Matthew would consume it. Usually, the old man grew more silent as dusk drew closer, but it didn't manifest as fatigue. Something about the setting sun quieted him, and although Matthew didn't know why, he knew enough to respect it. Charlie offered life; Leroy offered peace; and Matthew needed both.

He thought of the day's work ahead and his muscles twitched with anticipation. He was ready. Ready to sweat and ready to see how much progress they could make. Little by little, the wall was spreading across the outer limits of the estate—not unlike the walls around the castle. He'd always wanted to break them down; but that emotion felt too far away to wrangle, even if just for the reminiscence of it.

Matthew breathed in the smell of breakfast and sighed one of the most satisfied noises he'd ever heard himself make.

The day wasn't awaiting him; he was awaiting the day.

After breakfast and colorful conversation with Ezer, never short of stories from her home territory of Racham, Matthew wrapped a pastry in paper and pushed through the doors to the outside. He started his way across the field to join the men already working the wall. His feet carried him swiftly and lightly, knowing their way without guidance, and needing no motivation to move. He walked with purpose but not urgently, knowing the work ahead would be just enough.

A scream from the direction of the wall stopped his forward motion.

It was Charlie.

A rush of energy threw him into a sprint that brought him quickly to the wall, and to a scene that he was sure would never leave him. Charlie stood with his hands on the wall, bloody stripes growing across his small back. Rage filled Matthew's chest and threatened to choke him as his eyes hungrily searched for the deliverer of the blows. His ears rang out rebellion, closing them off to the sounds from the scene. In a pitch of fury and pause, he found him, barely noticed for lack of height or girth.

It was Sebastian.

Not five feet behind Charlie, Sebastian stood with a whip in a tender hand, holding a tool it knew not how to wield. Two keepers stood on either side of Sebastian, training humanity out of him.

One of them was the boy's father.

A WEEK LATER

Ezer dropped a plate of food in front of Matthew and sat next to him with a thud.

"Okay," she said, "enough."

Matthew didn't face her. He sat with his head in his hands staring at the table in front of him.

"It's been a week, child."

She waited, but Matthew didn't respond.

"Charlie's fine," she added, "and he misses you."

Finally, Matthew pulled his eyes up to meet hers.

"We will talk about this tonight. It's time to fix you."

She poked at the yellow that grew into his hair, but he knew she meant more than that. He knew he couldn't avoid her any longer. A hat would only disguise him for so long, and she wasn't going to give him a choice in the matter.

He met her in the same small room where they'd begun. She was there before him, arranging items on the metal table in the corner. She greeted him without turning around and told him to take his seat, her eccentricities fully in place. She methodically went to work on his head and spoke the one word she was going to offer with authority.

"Talk."

Ezer was the only person on the estate who knew who Matthew really was, and in this moment, he was glad she was the one who had sought him out. There were things to say that only she could hear, and an hour later, though her work on his head was far past complete, his words still rushed like water from a fall.

Matthew spoke of life in the castle, of his childhood—or lack thereof—and he spoke of the superiority he was taught to live by. He recalled the dictatorial nature of his father's rule, the still-aching loss of his mother, and of the faintest glimmer of life that Faith brought into his desert. Matthew shared his need to understand the exile, and of the guilt that followed him over what his family's throne had allowed. He spoke of the contentment he experienced at feeling like he finally belonged in Kolpisi, and the gnawing truth that his belonging was contingent upon a lie.

He wouldn't belong when they found out who he was. They would hate him.

The scene with Sebastian and his father woke a sleeping beast in Matthew. It was like watching his own childhood. Shame grew in him like a dark monster. If these people, his friends, the ones he considered his family, knew who he really was, they wouldn't accept him. He would be killed. Whether at the hands of the owners or the captives didn't matter. He'd kept the most foundational aspects of his identity hidden under fake dark hair and a closed mouth.

They didn't even use his given name—or know what it was, for that matter.

Ezer listened quietly, nodding her understanding, and requiring nothing. When his words trickled to a drip, Matthew's shoulders hunched in concession and exhaustion. Ezer rose from her chair and unlocked a drawer at the bottom of her table. After retrieving something from deep within the drawer, she returned and pulled up a chair to sit in front of him. Her knees pushed against his and she placed a maternal hand on one of his legs. She exhaled shortly before she began to speak.

"When I first caught wind of these," she said holding up a hand full of letters, "you were doin' real good here."

She half-smiled.

"You seemed happy... content. I didn't want to mess that up, so I thought better to wait." She raised her shoulders slightly. "Maybe I shouldn't have, I don't know."

She extended the envelopes to him.

"Jus' trying to protect you. Keep you happy."

She nodded at him once and left, closing the door behind her. By the light that still flickered in the room, Matthew found letters addressed to him. They were weathered, having traveled across Physis in search of their intended.

He slowly opened the one dated the earliest and by the time he got through a few more, silent tears flowed down a well-travelled path from his cobalt eyes to the corner of his chin. They slipped unhindered, down onto the last envelope in front of him, dotting it with moisture.

He opened it slowly, and let it finish what had already begun in him.

Matthew,
    Overthrow is imminent.
    If you receive this, hasten your return.
    We need you.
    I need you.
    - Faith

CHAPTER THIRTY-SIX

JONATHAN

The Physis Sea

In only ten days on the water, the fleet of Refuge ships already sailed together as one unit. Until Jude's leadership proved effective, council mandated the fleet stay together. When each respective crew and captain could demonstrate a compliance to the new rules, they would be permitted to spread out and cover more ground.

Jonathan wasn't worried. Jude was a natural leader. He had not only earned the respect of the fleet following him, but he was the one who had inspired them to take up their oars in the first place. The crews would do what was necessary to keep the mission alive. Jonathan was sure of it.

They were a common breed, restless and eager to have water under them again. For some of them, it was the nobility of the mission that mattered; for some, the thrill of the danger into which they rowed; but for most, it seemed, they were simply not made to live life in one place. If Jonathan related to any, it was the latter. But returning to the water would not be all pleasure.

Time apart from Collette had eased that ache, but Jonathan remembered what it felt like to work elbow to elbow with her. Although he was glad to welcome a more adept partner than his assistant on the Esperanza, he would have to work hard to keep the walls around his heart high. He knew Collette would notice, maybe she already did. Their comradery was not what it once was, and he was glad for it. It would be harder when they started bringing patients aboard, but for now, he would spend as much time as he could at the helm, letting the distance cushion him, and watching the rise and fall of the sun like it held his very soul.

"Brother," Jude said behind him.

Jonathan didn't turn to face Jude as he approached. He didn't need to. He kept his eyes on the horizon and lifted one hand to his brother's shoulder in a known greeting. Jude stood next to him silently, the two existing without effort.

Jonathan knew the arduous nature of Jude and Collette's decision to return to the water without Josie. He imagined Jude had put himself through a lot over the past few weeks, second-guessing every decision, analyzing and re-calculating every step. He knew Jude was likely reliving some of the terror of their last experience, remembering what it felt like to fear for the life of his wife around every corner. But Jonathan could see all the way through his friend, and he knew his processing didn't stop there.

Jude was also invigorated. His eyes sparkled and his step was quick. His orders were clear, and more authoritative than ever. He may have been content on Zoar, but he was made for *this*. And he was good at it. The Refuge fleet would accomplish more in a month than they had in the two years they were out the first time.

Although Jonathan could see and understand what Jude was experiencing, he didn't relate to him anymore. It was an unfamiliar feeling, to stand next to his closest friend, and not be able to understand him.

Jude had the perfect life in Zoar. Physis would and could exist without the Refuge mission. The war would continue as it always had, and although they would save a few lives here and there, Jonathan could not see how the mission was worth trading the life Jude left back in Zoar. It was the kind of life Jonathan knew he would never have, but the idea of willingly leaving it behind was something he could not grasp.

Although his body was still mending from the attack on the Esperanza, staying in Zoar was never an option for Jonathan. He remembered the day Jude announced his agreement with the council, and he knew the one thing he'd hoped to avoid would no longer be avoidable.

He would be working with Collette again. It would be his newest war, and one that promised some of the hardest work he would ever have to do.

But Jonathan belonged to the water, and he belonged with Jude and Collette. They were his family and there was no other place for him. On top of that, the peace he felt at the helm was something he found nowhere else, and he wouldn't trade it for anything.

When it came down to it, there was no decision to make. He was here again, with his brother beside him. He was okay.

He only hoped he would feel the same when the real work began.

CHAPTER THIRTY-SEVEN

JUDE

Water flew up from the ocean's surface and blinded Jude to the scene in front of him. The battle they'd sailed upon hours earlier was as violent as any they'd seen, and the sparring territories looked to be nowhere near closing their deadly aims.

Small Refuge skiffs darted in and out of warring water picking up bodies and carrying them back to the Refuge ships within range. Jude fought his instinct to order his own ship back from the fight, knowing he couldn't show special protection for the ship whose belly held Collette. The emotion threatened to drown him just as much as the angry water that surrounded him.

Jude muscled his focus back to the unrelenting task in front of him, clearing his eyes and directing his skiff to an unconscious solider nearby. It took three men to pull the lifeless body aboard, but at the discovery of a faint heartbeat, Jude ordered the skiff back to the Refuge.

The man rowing behind Jude was the first to notice.

"Captain, looks like we fished us a high ranker—a commander, maybe."

In between pulls, Jude took a quick glance at the unresponsive man on the floor behind him. Stripes on the man's uniform started at the shoulder and reached down past his elbow, signifying a great number of achievements. Pins on his collar harked the same. He'd lost his cap in the battle, but Jude concluded like the others, that this was an officer of a high rank.

"A life, just the same!" Jude shouted above the noise. "Pull!"

Approaching the Refuge, Jude could see flat beds dangling off its side for patients to be strapped in and lifted aboard. They approached and fastened the assumed commander into a flatbed. After he was lifted to the deck, Jude ordered the skiff back in the direction of the fighting, but shouts from the Refuge beckoned them to return. Crewmen from the deck of the Refuge waved him aboard, urging him back to their direction.

Many arduous pulls later, Jude worked one hand over the other as he climbed the ladder to the deck of the Refuge. His feet met the wooden deck with familiarity. At the push of a wave, the ship rocked, and he adjusted his balance. As the ship tilted, the red tide of water that ran across the wooden deck of the Refuge sloshed from bow to stern and across Jude's feet where he stood. The endless drag of bloodied men aboard kept the deck of the Refuge in a stained, persistent red. Though the ocean was many shades of blue in a day, the water on the Refuge never cleansed itself from crimson. The red tide rolled warmly over his feet and up to his ankles, the trademark of a day's work on the Refuge.

"Captain, the man you delivered, he's a commander."

"Yes," said Jude, somewhat agitated at the obviousness of it.

The crewman stared at Jude waiting for more, but Jude offered nothing.

"Is there anything else?" Jude asked.

Noise from the aft side diverted their conversation as a wailing solider was hoisted aboard. He was missing part of a foot and blood dripped from the wound, down onto the deck like honey off a comb. The push and pull of a wave washed the ruby tide again bringing the life of the wounded patient across the floor to the men who stood watching.

"Is this the Refuge?" the solider cried. "Am I on the Refuge?!"

Jude heard the man's voice lift in hope, and he watched as crewmen hoisted the soldier's flatbed for carriage to the infirmary.

The man nearest the solider answered him.

"You made it, mate. Welcome to the Refuge." He patted him on the shoulder encouragingly. "Let's get you to a healer."

Jude watched relief overcome the soldier's expression. His body relaxed into the flatbed that carried him, missing foot, and all.

Jude wondered at the man's response. He'd heard crewmen mention that the wounded were familiar with the Refuge, but he assumed the stories were exaggerated. This solider may have been nothing more than a screaming patient, but to Jude, he was proof of a miracle. The mission meant something. It was working. And it carried more than healing. It carried hope.

The crash of a cannonball into the side of a nearby ship sent debris in every direction.

"Captain! It's one of ours!" a crewman yelled.

Those on deck watched as their sister ship lost a majority part of her bow. Pieces of the vessel flew into the air and decorated the water surrounding it.

Jude watched the foreign attacker reload for a second round. His heart pounded at the thought that they could lose more than a ship today. The entire Refuge fleet was close enough to be impacted. Not to mention the lives of their crew—and all those receiving care below deck.

"Raise the white, Captain!" a crewman cried. He shouted to Jude from across the deck, helplessly watching the scene unfold along with the others.

Jude knew the act of raising a white flag would slow the attack but it would also lead to their fleet being boarded and stripped. With Collette below, that was a risk he was unwilling to take, so he acted on the only idea that came to mind.

"Bring me the white!" Jude ordered.

A crewman's sweating forearms wrestled a large white flag into Jude's hands. He flapped it outward, letting it catch the wind, and then lowered it carefully into the red tide at his feet. The lifeblood of every territory in Physis mixed into one common color.

Red stained through the white with the life spilt from those they saved... the very ones who shot at them.

Crimson-soaked and dripping to its ends, Jude ordered the red flag raised.

It held no emblem. No stripes or shapes. No loyalties. No allegiances. It was nothing more than the common color of life, seeped into a common thread, and raised to spare the spared and the sparing.

Skiffs carried the order to the others in the fleet, hoping the volume of ships raising red would be enough to deter a continued attack. No territory flew red. The presence of an unknown flag would quell the attack at least long enough for retreat.

"Ready the guns, Captain!"

A crewman voiced mankind's instinct, and eager eyes turned toward Jude, hungrily awaiting the order.

"We spare life!" Jude shouted. "We won't take it!"

Jude knew fear would consume them. He only hoped to slow it long enough to offer them a different choice.

"It requires much greater courage to stand still than it does to fight!"

Jude paused, wondering if he could push them past their instincts.

"Can you offer me that?!" he shouted.

CHAPTER THIRTY-EIGHT

COLLETTE

Collette heard the explosions from the infirmary. They were nearer than normal. Everyone knew it. Some patients were nervous, shaking in their beds while fear overcame them in sickening fogs. Others accepted it calmly, having welcomed their deaths long ago.

"Take us to Zoar!" the patient yelled. "Sail on!"

It had been his constant request since being brought aboard. He'd bled from both eyes upon his arrival and hadn't regained his vision yet. Collette wasn't sure if he would. But he didn't need his sight to know the battle was closing in. And it made even more urgent his cries.

"Take us to Zoar! Please!" he urged.

He was not alone. Many of the patients begged for deliverance to Zoar. To Collette's surprise, the Refuge reputation had spread all over Physis in the last years.

More surprising though, was the divide among its audience. For every patient relieved to be rescued by the

Refuge, two or three strained against it. Some refused treatment. Some begged to be released and sent back to the war—regardless the severity of their injuries. Some even asked for the mercy of a brief end to avoid the shame of being convalesced on the Refuge.

It was one such patient that called her by a name she never expected.

Traitor.

And it wasn't just her. It's what they called all the Refuge crew. In their eyes, the mission went against the progress of the war and only prolonged it. In their eyes, a neutral territory was an enemy to all and a friend to none.

The collision of the two parties made the infirmary a bridge near breaking in every moment. Collette found herself relieved when a demonstrative patient would fall under, regardless of which side of the line he fell on. She yearned for silence, so the peace below deck might return. People in Physis were born to hate anyone from a territory different than their own. The added, contentious layer of the Refuge mission made the balance even more tedious.

Collette was glad the people below were injured. Not because she wanted them to suffer, but because it was the only thing keeping them from their own additional war below deck. She was nervous every time a new patient came through the door. What used to hold the thrill of healing now caused her stomach to flip every time the door swung open.

And the door had been unrelenting in the past few days. She found herself near sick and dragging with fatigue at every task. Jonathan worked ceaselessly beside her, saying near nothing, and burying himself in whatever problem came through the door.

She knew the experience on the Esperanza had changed him, but it wasn't until the work started that she really saw it. His face was the same. His body recovered. But he wasn't there; and she didn't know why. She observed him inconspicuously from across the infirmary floor, wondering what could snap him out of it and bring him back.

A stir from a cot nearby broke Collette's observation of Jonathan and drew it to her waiting patient.

When the soldier arrived, he was unconscious and carrying more water in his lungs than a fish. Her diagnosis was broken ribs and a fractured clavicle. When he regained consciousness, he thrashed against her efforts to help him, wounding himself further. In his delirium he proclaimed the greatness of Gaon, naming it the future of Physis, and laying claim to its superiority over all else. He was loud and proud and passionate—all the trademarks of Gaon's long-held reputation.

Collette sighed with disappointment at his awakening and prepared herself for the fight. She approached him just as his newest protest began.

"No! No! No!" he shouted. "No! Gaon will not take refuge! We will not take refuge!"

He tore at the covers around him as Collette neared. She was thankful that her arrival quieted him, even if it was just temporary. She placed her hand softly on his arm and tried to smile at him.

"Gaon will not take refuge," he said, quieter this time.

"Sir, you have broken ribs and a broken clavicle," Collette said, softly touching where his breaks were.

His venom returned in a bite. "Release me! I command it!"

"We have no prisoners here." Collette lifted a hand to the door. "If you can walk, you may go."

At her words, the patient jerked to rise from his cot and was instantly defeated by the pain that overtook him. Collette nodded at him knowingly, her hands resting easily in her pockets.

"Okay," she said trying to hide a smirk, "now that we have that out of the way. There's water next to you if you decide you want it and I'll be back to check on you in a little while."

He offered her a scowl and she left, relieved to service a less combative patient.

ONE WEEK LATER

Collette sighed, exasperated. "Aadi, take the medicine. You will sleep better and heal faster."

"It's *Commander* Aadi," he corrected.

His disposition hadn't changed much in the last week, except that he was a little stronger and a little more stubborn than when he first arrived.

"Yes, I know, *Commander*." She added a sarcastic emphasis in a way she knew he wouldn't miss. "Everyone knows that you are a commander, and we are all very impressed."

"Everyone except for you," he said plainly.

She chuckled at his quip. He was correct.

"Take the medicine," she said.

She was growing weary of this game. He'd made it clear that he wanted to depart the Refuge. Gaon was not a territory keen on accepting help. They did not support the efforts of the mission, and as Commander Aadi liked to remind her, "Gaon will rule Physis."

Collette could not count the number of times he'd repeated the line to her over the last few days. He may have been ashamed to be there, but his body was not offering him the strength to leave—despite his valiant efforts.

"Why do you even bother?" he said, crippled by resentment.

"Because if you take your medicine, you will sleep better and heal faster," she extended the medicine to him again. "And then you can leave, and I won't have to deal with you anymore," she added, cheerfully.

"No," he shook his head. "No. Why do you bother fishing

half-dead men out of the sea?" He closed his eyes and let his head fall back to his pillow. "The point of war is death," he continued, "do you really think you can stop it?"

She stood next to him, her hands unsure of what to do without the permission to see to his care. Most of her time spent with the commander involved her standing over him and arguing over his need for care—a task she'd been unsuccessful at achieving thus far.

"Stop the war?" Collette asked. "No, even we are not *that* hopeful."

She looked at him thoughtfully hoping her words, Mae's words, would mean something to him.

"We started our mission—and continue it—on one very simple belief." She looked squarely into him. "That the most valuable human life, is one with a beating heart inside his chest."

She placed a hand gently on his chest.

"And in this moment, *Commander*, that human is you."

She watched his forehead crinkle in response and shrugged her shoulders.

"And now your moment is over and it's that guy's turn."

She smiled at him smartly and began to turn away, but the proud smile that spread across his expression stopped her and pulled her back. She waited for his response, knowing he had one.

"You know we're the ones who attacked your boyfriend's ship."

His voice was low and proud, and he tipped his chin toward Jonathan when he said it.

"Yes, I know," she said.

Jonathan had recognized the territory's flag on the commander the moment he dragged him through the door. He knew it was the territory of Gaon who nearly shred the Esperanza to nothing that day. He knew it was likely the commander who gave the order that killed so many of the

Esperanza's crewmates.

In that moment, Collette chose to respond to Commander Aadi the same way she'd responded to Jonathan when he realized who the commander was:

"Doesn't change the mission," she said.

She looked into the uncomprehending eyes of the commander, smiled unapologetically, and walked away.

CHAPTER THIRTY-NINE

MATTHEW

Kolpisi

With Ezer's help, escape from the estate came easy.

Early in his captivity, Matthew spent hours dreaming of escape, mapping his way out of Kolpisi so he could get back to his pursuit of the mystery his mother left him in Zoar. But somewhere along the way, he grew past the need to pursue that life, and with it, he'd lost the desire to leave. He'd accepted his circumstances. He'd welcomed a fresh start. He'd given up the need for a way out long ago.

Fortunately for him, Ezer never did.

Thirty-three years on the plantation and she still hadn't stopped planning her own escape. She still wouldn't release the dream to return to her family in Racham. Her position inside the house provided just the right information. She knew when the delivery wagons were in and out of the estate. She knew their routes like she knew her reflection. She had a perfect plan for how to sneak onto one, and more importantly, she knew when and how they would be searched.

In one detailed tutorial, Matthew had a thorough, carefully planned escape route that only required an able body—the one thing Ezer did not have.

When she embraced him in goodbye, she dropped a tiny bag into his hands. In it were the three diamonds she'd cut from his neck.

"It's time to be who you are," she whispered.

She shaved his head, tucked a cap in his pocket, kissed him on the cheek, and pushed him out the door, giving one final review of the plan.

For the entirety of the shaky ride to the docks at the Aftodia Marketplace, Matthew allowed nothing to enter his mind except the repeated instructions of Ezer's plan. He chanted them over and over, filling his mind with nothing but the present like a mantra. If he stopped to think for a moment, he knew he would jump out of the wagon and forever abandon his life in the Diamond Isles.

But Faith needed him. And he was living a lie in Kolpisi.

"It's time to be who you are."

Matthew let Ezer's words repeat over and over in his mind. There was only one choice to make.

Matthew didn't let himself think about what he was leaving behind until he'd already set sail for Triton. Then he let himself agonize over it, welcoming regret at leaving his only family in Kolpisi. He reminded himself that they didn't know him at all and that they would undoubtedly reject him when they discovered it. The truth was that he had no home. He had no family. He didn't know who he was.

Matthew remembered being locked away below deck those years ago and thinking that those would be the darkest his days would ever know. But this was far darker. This was a midnight he could not see through.

He sailed between two worlds of glass. Both would shatter with truth. One of them was just days away from it.

Matthew wrestled with the realization that as much as he

longed to belong, he didn't.

He didn't belong to either world. In the first world—the isles—he should belong but didn't. In the newer world—Kolpisi—he shouldn't belong, but he felt like he did, almost. But only insofar as deceit could carry him.

What would Charlie think of him when he found out? How could Leroy not feel betrayed?

Matthew couldn't go back now. The damage was done.

The only way now was forward. Forward into the life he'd fled.

TRITON

When Triton appeared on the horizon, Matthew expected to feel a dread at what awaited him—a pecking nervousness in the very least. But curiosity took over, pushing aside every other emotion, forcing them to wait their turns.

The streets were empty; the mines quiet; the air still. The scene in front of him sat in stark contrast to his first visit years ago.

People had crowded in then, pushing against the royal guard. The noises had overwhelmed him so much that he'd heard nothing, the sounds combining into inaudible snow. Now, silence filled the space from cloud to ground, demanding deference for its stillness, and holding Matthew's attention in an unyielding grasp.

Greyness blanketed Triton in varying shadows and covered it as an overdue authority, home at long last. The few people Matthew passed didn't raise their eyes to meet him but stared blankly at the space in front of them. Trash littered the ground, sprinkling the scene in front of him in a presentation of disregard.

The content of Faith's letters sprang to his mind, sending

his stomach into the nervous knots he'd anticipated earlier. If this is what Triton looked like, what would he find in the isles?

A man sat on the dock where Matthew would board his last passage. The man sat with his back hunched and let two lifeless feet dangle over the dock's end.

"Ay, there," Matthew said, his colloquial skills far evolved from his last attempt.

The man remained, offering nothing more than a pull of the cigarette he lifted to his mouth.

Matthew continued anyway. "Will there be passage to the isles?"

Matthew bent slightly, attempting to catch the man's attention. The man dragged on his cigarette again and lifted the burning end in the direction of a fishing vessel nearby.

It was enough.

Matthew started on his way but turned to inquire again.

"Ay," he said, knowing he was pushing his luck. "What happened here?"

Finally, the man turned his eyes to Matthew. The fullness of their grey matched the air around them, blending him into it in a ghost-like blur. It was hard to decipher what emotion passed through the man, but eye contact was an improvement over the blankness that covered every other person he'd come across.

The man held Matthew's gaze for a pregnant moment before squishing his cigarette into the cracked wood next to him. He offered no more than one unsettling word.

"Mutiny."

The closer they got to the isles, the louder Matthew's heart thudded in his ears.

Dusk was upon them, and the dimming light cast an eerie glow to the sky that covered him.

Mutiny.

It carried an ambiguity that sat on his chest and made it hard to fill his lungs.

He never understood the way of life that separated one from another—the idea of "us" and "them" always pushing against his instinct. There was a part of him that hoped a disruption would come to his world, but it wasn't until now, with the isles nearing with every pull of the oars, that he realized *he* should have been the disruption.

It should have been his objective from the start. He was the one with the leverage. He was the to-be king. If he would have listened to his mother, he could have learned how to change the system from the inside out. He could have changed it all. He could have rewritten the rules, pushed back against the standard. It was all right at his fingertips.

But instead, he'd run away.

When Matthew was sold, he welcomed resentment like a well-earned badge, allowing it to cover him with self-concern. Bitterness toward his father ate at him. He'd laid stone after stone ruminating on his hate, when he could have been here, in his home, preventing the overthrow of the throne. He'd spent his time detesting the one thing that held the power to make the changes they needed... and by choosing to leave, he sacrificed it all.

Regret slithered from his feet, up to his knees, and into his stomach and neck until it felt like it might choke him.

Did his father survive the overthrow? Would Matthew find him alive, tortured, imprisoned? What about Faith? What if her family had to flee? How would he find her if they had to leave the isles? Would she be angry that he took so long to return? Could she care for him still when she found out he'd willingly stayed away and claimed a new life for himself?

Matthew focused his attention on the deck of the boat below his feet until the fisherman poked him to acknowledge their arrival. The fisherman rubbed together cracking, cold fingers and awaited payment before shooing Matthew off deck to begin his work for the night.

Matthew made his way down the docks and cleared the small hill that brought the rest of the isles into view.

Destruction.

It was the only word that could describe it. It met him unapologetically, and in more forms than Matthew knew existed. From the closest blade of grass to the furthest edges of land, estates were decimated, burned down, or plowed through. The word "Triton" was painted on every surface flat enough to make it legible. Debris from the annihilation covered the ground as a grass of its own kind, unforgiving in sight and drastically limiting mobility.

Although his instinct was to run to Faith's family estate, the tediousness of travelling around the debris made travel too hard and too dangerous. The obliterated nature of the once-familiar scene made it hard to keep his wits about him, causing him to lose his bearings and his balance more than once.

When he finally pinpointed where he was, he'd long passed Faith's property and was near where the castle should be.

He was glad for the preparation of seeing the rest of the isles before reaching the castle. The walls around the royal estate had been blasted down into bits. It was hard to identify what instrument could have done the damage, but the walls that once stood high and proud were nothing more than piles of defeated rock, no more than common in their every essence.

Only small parts of the castle remained intact, a tower here and there, and a part of the main body of the building. Faith's letter stated that most of the royal guard was gone before the attacks started. She had warned Matthew that if they were attacked, there wouldn't be much protection remaining for his father.

The lump in his throat grew, though he wasn't sure if he feared facing his father, or his father's death, more.

Matthew made his way through what used to be the front of the castle and climbed over piles of rock before coming to a wing of the building that appeared most intact. To his surprise, he found the east wing much like it was the day he left. The high ceilings remained, the walls stood firmly in place, and paintings and wall décor hung just where his mother had requested them so many years ago.

Matthew worked his way around, wondering at the seemingly pristine nature of his surroundings, so juxtaposed to the rest of what he'd seen. The faint clanging of dishes caught his attention and turned his eyes down the corridor in which he stood. He wondered if it was only a memory of the sound down the hall that caused his ears to hear it, but soon the drifting smell of roasted duck lifted his nose and sharply focused his senses.

He was not imagining or remembering the sensation of dinner down the hall—it was happening. Now. Dinner was in progress.

He slowed his walk to avoid ancillary noise and adjusted his position to protect himself from being seen. He strained his ears hoping to catch any of the indistinct conversation coming from the dining room but could not make it out without getting closer. He continued slowly down the hall, limiting his breaths to what was necessary until he made out the sound of his father's voice.

Matthew stepped slowly around a corner that brought his father into view, looking more normal than ever. There sat the king, at the head of his grand table, adorned with his crown, and attentively consuming a plate of delicately garnished food before him.

Matthew relaxed at the sight. It was somehow relieving to see his father acting so much like himself in the middle of the catastrophe. It was a manifestation of irony, and yet perfectly standard for the king, seated at his decadent table with fine food and drink, while the very walls around him crumbled.

It was so standard, in fact, it was almost boring.

Matthew let out a sigh of sarcastic contempt and shook his head at the scene. He rose out of his crouched position against the wall and came around the corner into the full view of the dining room, ready to casually announce his return to his unconcerned father.

But as the rest of the room came in view, Matthew stopped short and froze. He adjusted his eyes to confirm it. He knew coming here that he would have to prepare himself for the unknown, but in his most horrific visions of what he would face he never imagined the sight in front him.

At the end of the dining table, opposite the king, in his mother's chair, sat the epitome of elegance and grace. A refined woman, dressed in the royal robe and crown, the very essence of regality in a well-manicured package. The new queen.

Faith.

CHAPTER FORTY

COMMANDER AADI

The sea air felt welcoming to him, like home after a long trip away. The skiff moved at a strong pace, pushing the breeze against his face in a familiar embrace. He adjusted his jacket around him, pushing and pulling it into the place it used to fit.

He breathed in as fully as he could, his lungs still lousy after the battle a near month ago. The healing had come slowly—much slower than he hoped. Every day on the Refuge was a day he would have to explain, not only to his men, but to the Vice Admiral as well.

Gaon was unbending in its position regarding the mission. The fact that Commander Aadi had received treatment and been released back to his territory would not be welcomed. The more honorable action would have been to end his own life, along with the lives of those onboard the Refuge. He was concerned about how he would be received by his people, and it tightened around his shoulders and neck, making him stiffer than he already was. He would push it from his mind.

Allowing himself to consider the possibilities would only make him anxious, and that was simply not acceptable.

He forced his shoulders back and extended his chest out as far as he could hold it. In the least, he would present himself as a commander to his troops.

He would refuse to let them see anything but that.

Gaon's fleet floated into sight and Commander Aadi watched Refuge crewmen set down their oars to raise the white for their approach to the fleet. Aadi stood erect, one foot hoisted on the bench in front of him. He fought against the instinct to lean on his knee in response to the pain perched under his ribs.

"Commanders don't lean. No Gaon soldier would," he coached himself.

Murmurs spread across the deck as his native crew began to recognize their lost commander. They dutifully assumed positions of respect, lowering their hats, and saluting their returned leader.

A faint relief teased him, and he wondered if all would be forgiven for his recovery on the enemy ship, but his tenure told him better. It would not be that simple. Not by Gaon's measure.

The Refuge skiff carried him flush against the side of the Gaon vessel he would board. Refusing additional help, Commander Aadi grabbed the ladder that was carved into the side of the ship and began his ascent. It wasn't as easy as he hoped it would be, but he did it, nonetheless, denying pain a home in his body.

When his feet were on deck, he fought a surprising urge to wave goodbye to the Refuge crew who had carried him there. But he would not. He *could* not. He did not turn around to acknowledge their effort or departure, but kept his eyes trained ahead.

"Commander," his mate saluted him. "The Vice Admiral awaits."

Commander Aadi saluted back and followed the soldier. He didn't know what awaited him, but he knew he could do what he was trained to do. No emotion would surface; he would obey whatever order came; and he would offer no excuse for receiving aid from the enemy.

He would face the consequences for his choice with honor, no matter the cost.

Commander Aadi entered the Vice Admiral's quarters expecting questions as to why he was returning on a Refuge skiff. More directly, he expected to be asked why he didn't take the vessel down while he had the opportunity. He expected to be accused of treason, to be demoted, and to be commanded to do the dutiful thing he was trained to do—end his life with honor.

But none of that happened. None of it at all.

Upon entering the Vice Admiral's chambers, he came upon his leader, and several other commanders and colonels, in the midst of planning Gaon's next attack. They all stood around a table, discussing which tactics may be the most successful. The Vice Admiral hardly raised his eyes from the table. He only waved Commander Aadi near with a quick hand through the air.

"Commander, come," the Vice Admiral said.

It was as if he'd never been gone. It was as if the past month was a dream, his injuries caused by nothing more than crooked sleep. The ache that interrupted his every inhale told him otherwise.

While the officers strategized around the table, Commander Aadi worked to quell rising emotion down into his gut. He wanted to shake acknowledgement into the men in the room, and shout at them that he was ready to face his punishment. He wanted to scream the acceptance of his fate to earn back the honor he'd lost.

Instead, he walked quietly to the table, not quite fitting between the men who stood around it anymore. He angled in sideways so he could see the strategy board, one foot in toward the table, and one turned outward, away from the group.

For the first time in his memory, he felt out of place. Awkward.

Commander Aadi listened to what the men said and nodded along when they came to agreement. He straightened in salute to accept the role he would play in the next attack.

He welcomed the idea of returning to battle. If the Vice Admiral wouldn't allow him a rightful punishment, he would make a display of his loyalty in the next best way he knew how—by the sword.

TWO DAYS LATER

The battle happened quickly. Before Commander Aadi could clear out the internal mud. In a blink he was fighting again, shouting commands at his men like nothing had changed.

Except, everything had.

His orders weren't clear. He couldn't remember the strategy. He hesitated at every decision. He questioned every instinct. Again, and again, he raised his weapon to strike and lowered it clean. It was as if a cloud was set before his eyes and no one else's. The way was clear to all the rest of them, but he felt blind. The battle felt like a still frame—a song, unbearably slow.

He knew the Vice Admiral's grace would not last. After not receiving a proper punishment for his betrayal, and now missing the opportunity to atone for his sins in battle, he would most certainly come to the end of the line. Or, even worse, what if the Vice Admiral continued his silence? What if he continued not to acknowledge Aadi's absence, his return, or his acceptance of the Refuge's aid?

Whichever of the two fates was coming, Commander Aadi knew he could not endure it.

After the battle, he'd fallen into his cot, exhausted. His body was not recovered from his injuries and the effects of it severely limited his endurance. He stared at the ceiling above him, trying to relive moments of the battle and envision himself performing as he should have. He tried to see the plan and hear himself shout the right commands at the right times. He tried to picture his men responding to him like the machine they once were.

But he couldn't see anything. His memory couldn't retrieve clear enough pictures to inform even a fantasized improvement. He rubbed his eyes hoping to clear his mind, and then let his body fall into another restless sleep.

Collette appeared over him, smirking.

She reminded him of his daughter. Sassy, and yet undyingly kind. He tried not to let it affect a softness for her, but it did, and he knew it.

She offered him water and said, "the most valuable human is one with a beating heart inside his chest."

He felt her pat his shoulder lightly as he swallowed, and he laid his head on the pillow below him. He was nearly settled when the pillow slipped, and he fell...

He hit the floor, shaking himself out of an already fitful sleep.

He rubbed the back of his neck and sat up on the floor. The number of unsuccessful nights of sleep were piling up. His eyes burned with unrest and his body ached with complaint, but he knew there was no more use in trying tonight.

He painfully lifted himself off the floor of his quarters and dressed for the night air. Once above deck, Commander Aadi paced the starboard side watching the water push along the side of a ship that used to feel familiar.

Discontent flooded him from the ground up and he walked continuously, hoping to quiet it. He stomped on the feeling with every stride, forcing it deeper inside him until its voice muffled somewhere inside his gut.

If sleep couldn't quiet his tossing soul, he would walk until the sun itself broke over the horizon and cut through the darkness.

CHAPTER FORTY-ONE

ISSACHAR

Agon

Issachar observed Eden from afar, doing everything he could to avoid her noticing his gaze. He knew she had probably already seen him checking up on her every few hours, stalking around the corners where she studied and taught.

Part of him didn't care that she caught him. He was the chief, and more importantly, he was her father. But another part of him didn't want to upset her any further than he already had. He missed her warm greetings and embrace. He missed easily conversing with her and knowing her loyalty would always lie with him. Losing his eldest daughter to the man she'd fallen in love with was a transition Issachar knew could not be avoided long-term.

But having been the person to send that man to the warfront before his time... Issachar didn't know if Eden would ever forgive him for that.

In truth, he was just as upset with himself as he was with her. He couldn't believe he didn't notice her actions sooner. He had blindly believed her deceit. He'd dismissed her odd behavior time and time again. Was he too self-concerned? His daughter had trained as a warrior right under his nose, using his own weapons, and by a secret lover.

He had failed. Not only as a father, but as a chief. And all at once.

Amafis should have had another year to train in Agon before leaving for the warfront. He was an adept warrior, well-versed in war strategy, and a skilled fighter. But he was still green in a battle, and everyone knew it. He was at high risk on the warfront.

Given other circumstances, Issachar may have supported the match, proud to pair his first daughter with such a fine warrior. As it was, Issachar fumed at the idea that Amafis successfully fostered deceit with her. Not only that, but he simultaneously broke Agonian law by training a woman by the sword.

In a different time, Amafis would have been forced to engage in single combat against the chief as a way of penance. Lucky for him, Agon could not afford to lose an able fighter to a friendly blade, no matter the reason.

Instead, Issachar decided that Amafis would join the first early deployment. It would suffice for his punishment. It would hurt Eden as much as it did the young man, and Issachar was beginning to wonder if the choice punished himself most of all.

Issachar watched Eden correct the young girl she worked with, undoing her stitching, and resetting it for her to try again. Her long, dark fingers worked the cloth with agility and grace, just ask they did against the piano, or when she carefully garnished a plate at dinner.

The idea of her beauty and delicacy wielding a weapon to end a man's life felt as ill-suited as a bull dancing. It simply wasn't right. Issachar could not accept it.

Eden's tightly curled hair grew wild around her eyes and

brought out the midnight set behind them. She was the essence of femininity, a careful balance of strength and grace. What drove her instincts to join the ranks of the warrior, he would never understand.

Apart from obligatory greetings, Eden had not spoken to Issachar since the deployment. Their interactions were minimal, and he imagined they would continue that way. That much he'd expected.

What he didn't expect was the affront from the people of Agon.

Agon was the warrior territory. Its heritage of great physical authority in Physis marked its title and extended its legend to the ends of the sea. Parents birthed sons desiring them to be the greatest fighters among their peers, pushing them in training and coaching them through war tactic like parents sing lullabies to babies.

But when the call came to ready their sons for early departure, rumblings rose like from the base of a mighty volcano.

Some accepted the order as plainly as any other, but most were shaken with the novelty of the new command. The uniqueness of the order gave exposure to the true vulnerability Agon faced, and its citizens saw right through it.

Issachar should have known they would.

The people were beginning to question his honesty as their leader. Issachar wondered if they also questioned their loyalty to him. For the first time, public criticism openly rained down on him.

Urgent footsteps echoed down the stone corridor and interrupted Issachar's observations of Eden. Jonas was approaching quickly.

"Chief, you're needed—now."

The tone in Jonas' voice was new. Issachar couldn't place it. He matched Jonas' rapid pace into a small, windowless room.

Historically, this was a room used only for the most confidential of conversations. During Issachar's leadership, it hadn't been used at all.

Jonas pushed the door shut behind them before locking it from the inside. Only three men stood around the table. Jonas was the first to speak.

"Chief, Dante has just arrived from the north."

Eagerness. That's what Issachar heard behind Jonas' voice.

"Triton has overthrown the Diamond Isles," Jonas said excitedly.

Shocked, Issachar looked from Jonas to Dante, astounded.

"It cannot be true," he said.

Dante stood with his hat in his hand. The short-statured man had been a scout for Agon since he could sail on his own.

"It's true. Saw it with my own eyes. The castle is down. They took out everything. No sign of the royal guard anywhere."

Issachar placed both hands on the table in front of him and tried to process what he'd just heard. The Century War was a balance of the fight between these two superpowers. One would take an advantage and then the other, striking and then retreating but making no measurable progress over the other. Other territories may nibble at the scraps, but the war rested on these two: the Diamond Isles and Agon. The taker would ultimately rule Physis, and everyone knew it.

One hundred and fifty years into the war and new generations still fought over dead men's disagreements. Occasionally Issachar had wondered why and how the fighting started, but he grew to believe it wasn't his job to know. It was his job to uphold the legacy of Agon, and he was committed to it—no matter the cost.

As Issachar stood considering the news, he saw the biggest advantage that had come to pass in 150 years, and it had fallen into *his* lap. If they could take out the isles before anyone else, Agon could own control over all Physis. They could put order to the rest of the world—order that had helped them thrive as a territory for all these years. Most importantly, they could set up fair trade systems, so they could stop having to protect so fiercely what they had.

This was the key to the power. It was the key to improving their world. They had to take it.

But Issachar's fantasy was not long-lived.

"We can't," he said. "We have no men to take it," he realized aloud.

The irony of the qualm felt like poison in his blood. At every other point in their history, Agon would have had fleets of men ready to depart, but now, when the moment of opportunity had finally come, they had no one to send. Citizens would revolt at the idea of launching another early deployment, and they didn't have one prepared to send anyhow.

"Where are their ships?" Issachar asked Dante, but Jonas answered before the scout could.

"They're not within sight of the isles. It's our belief that their troops have not yet received word of the mutiny."

That was all Issachar needed.

"Jonas, you will lead them," he ordered.

"Chief, I cannot," Jonas answered grimly.

"You can, and you will," Issachar affirmed.

Agon's first focus was always to protect its resources, people, and homeland. It was the chief's primal duty to stay and protect the home and the people—not to lead offensive attacks against their enemies. Jonas knew that. They all did. It made Jonas the only suitable choice for an attack.

"In due respect, chief, this is too great an opportunity." Jonas continued, "the Diamond Isles will not expect you. They may ready for attack, but they will not be prepared for an attack by the Agonian chief and his team. You must be the one. Take your guard and make Physis ours."

The men around the table pounded their agreement into

the frame before them.

Issachar had to admit, the thrill of the take made his heart pound with anticipation. The loss of the ecstasy of battle was the tradeoff to accepting the role as chief. Issachar would only ever see a real battle again if they were attacked on their own soil, and that was a far-off possibility until a month ago.

He missed the adrenaline that overtook him and the animalistic life lived inside a warrior's skin. He missed the thump of his heart inside his ears and the liberating feeling of letting his body control the rest of him.

Issachar knew a victory like this would win him back the favor of the people of Agon—and maybe even Eden's along with it. Everything would be different if they took the isles.

"Very well," he consented. "Jonas will remain."

Jonas nodded his affirmation, seeming to have expected Issachar's concession. Issachar locked eyes with Jonas.

"You are the acting chief in Agon until I return," he said. "Prepare the men."

Blood filled the veins on the back of his thick hands and drove itself up, thumping wildly into his neck, coursing its way back home.

"We leave at dawn."

CHAPTER FORTY-TWO

COLLETTE

The Physis Sea

"You have to tell him."

Collette emptied the last contents of her stomach into a bedpan. She could feel the gentle adjustment of Jonathan's hands on the bundle of hair he held up and out of her way.

"You have to tell him," he repeated.

Collette narrowed her eyes at his words. She knew she had to tell him. Everything in her wanted to tell him. But the memory of her last announcement cautioned her otherwise. She remembered how excited she had been to share the news and how she anticipated his joy at the celebration they would share over the life growing inside her.

But that's not how it happened at all.

Instead, fear pooled in the bottoms of his eyes, and he shook on the ground where he stood. Alarm spread across his face like a slow-growing omen and urgency set his feet to the task of returning her to Zoar. Nothing mattered to him until the day he set her feet on dry land, and that was then.

The stakes were higher now.

Now, an entire fleet depended on Jude's guidance and attention. Seven ships filled with beating hearts. They needed him sharp. They needed him present. They needed him engaged in the mission.

Collette was sure the news she carried would make him incapable of any of it.

They'd only been back on the water for three months, and three months matched her calculations. Maybe it happened on the early days on the water before they reached the battles. Maybe it happened before they set sail, in those last, easy, dreamlike days on the island. By her deduction, they were only a few months' sail from Zoar, and she promised herself if they got any further away, she would tell him. In the worst case, Jonathan could deliver the baby onboard. She knew the concern wasn't much about the baby being delivered onboard as much as it was for the safety of a mismatched family on the Physis Sea.

If it had to be done, it could be. Jude wouldn't like it, but it could be.

When Collette weighed her options, it was easy to see. She would rather have an onboard delivery than have Jude lose the opportunity to pass off the mission to a new leader. Just a few more months on the water would be enough for the council to see that the fleet could follow their new rules; and that they could do it independent of Jude. Then they could go home. Then they could be with Josie. Then they could return to their contented days in the Western Bay.

She knew she had to tell him, but the infrequency with which they saw each other was making the news easy to delay. The multiplied fleet and increased responsibilities kept them far from each other most days, unnoticed, and unattended.

But now, three months along, every day that passed made her surer he would not receive the news well. It came down to one very simple fact: every day he didn't know, was a day they were closer to returning, successful. Every day he didn't know, was a day closer to returning to Josie—for good. They couldn't abandon the mission early. If they did, he would have to return to complete it and she knew there would be no return for her.

Leaving Josie behind was the hardest thing she'd ever done. She wouldn't survive it a second time, especially with another child to consider.

There was no choice. They had to stay on the water. It was the only way. Jude had to remain in the dark, at least for now.

Keeping a common secret with Jonathan seemed to help mend the bridge between them. It may have been the only thing that kept him speaking to her, but it was enough. His constant attention and care forced him to communicate, and she was thankful—even if it did seem forced most days.

Some days, tending to her was the only time Jonathan looked her in the eyes. She tried not to take the distance personally. The combination of losing his mother, followed by his traumatic experience on the Esperanza had to be difficult for him. She wished he would talk about it. She hated watching him walk around half-alive.

"Tell him," Jonathan said again.

She wiped her mouth and shook her head at him.

"Not yet."

Jonathan sighed audibly. He crossed his muscular arms, painted with pictures of personalized significance, and leaned back onto the cabinet behind him.

"If you don't tell him, I'm going to, and believe me Collette, he will want to have heard it from you."

"Yes, Doctor," she said.

She rolled her eyes and pushed Jonathan out of her way so she could get to the supplies behind him.

"Let's go. We have patients to see."

THREE WEEKS LATER

Collette lay next to Jude in bed, lost in the comfort of remembering what it felt like to look her love in the eyes. It was the first time they'd been alone, awake, and in the same place in weeks. The quietness of the sea was a friend remembered, and she let herself sink into both it and Jude, forgetting, for a moment, the secret that quivered under her skin. She lingered in the ease of forgetfulness, and floated there, for just a moment too long.

She felt Jude's wandering hand stop abruptly on her belly and watched him as he cocked his head to one side. She recognized the look that spread across his face and prepared herself for the aftershock.

"Collette?" he asked, his voice rising.

She nodded.

"How long? I mean, I haven't even seen you since..." he trailed off, counting off on his fingers his own calculation.

"No!" His eyes widened. "Collette!"

He stood abruptly, immediately pacing the small space of their cabin's quarters.

"Four months? Four months!"

"I—" she tried to speak, but he cut her off.

"Tomorrow," he said, anger visibly filling his pores. He looked her directly in the eyes. "We leave tomorrow."

Collette thought about following him after he crashed out of their cabin, but she knew him well enough to know he needed time. He would have to process before he could talk about it rationally.

It's how he did things. He would be back. But not tonight.

CHAPTER FORTY-THREE

JUDE

All Jude could see was the door in front of him. He rushed for it, knowing escape was the only way he would avoid regretting his words later. He needed air. Space. Time.

Minutes earlier he'd felt exhausted, like sleep would overtake him the moment he let it. But now, adrenaline rushed through him and set his every fiber on fire.

He knew this feeling well, and just what to call it.

It was fear.

Jude hated admitting it. He didn't want to address it. For now, he just wanted to let it rush through his body and take over. He wanted to drown in it. Drowning in it would be easier than facing it. And face it he would—he would have to.

But for now, for just a few minutes, he let the fear swallow him.

His legs furiously drove him above deck. Darkness enveloped the sea, the new moon offering no light to the black around him. It closed in and matched him like nothing else could.

He was Zoarian. He always would be. But tonight, he felt more like his blood roots. He knew the stories. They were warriors. And he knew, deep down, he was as well. His life with Mae wrote a different narrative for his life, but tonight he was all Agon. And it felt good. In the blindness of it, he didn't see Jonathan approach, but he turned abruptly toward the sound when he heard it.

"Brother?" Jonathan asked.

Jude turned away to pace the deck, trying to wrangle his emotions.

"Jude?" Jonathan said again.

Jonathan's raised voice caused Jude's feet to stop. His hands grasped the sides of his head like they could somehow hold him together. The still of the night was interrupted only by the creak of the ropes on the masts and the cadence of the tide against the ship.

Jonathan could help. He always knew what to say. He was a constant source of calm, and he'd been a great advocate to Jude the last time this happened. Jonathan had pushed for their return to Zoar just as urgently as Jude did. Telling Jonathan was a good idea. He was going to find out anyway. Jude lassoed his wild eyes to meet his friend's.

"Collette is pregnant," Jude managed through a tight voice.

He wasn't sure how he expected Jonathan to respond. Maybe he would be empathetic. Maybe he would be as mad as Jude. Maybe he would be just as afraid. At least by telling him, Jude would have someone on his side. Someone who understood.

Jude's words hung in the air as he waited for Jonathan to respond. Was he shocked silent? It was hard to tell in the dark, but as Jude studied his friend's face, what he found betrayed him.

It was *relief*—and it gave Jonathan away like a spoiled present.

"You knew," Jude said flatly.

The Agonian roots that bore Jude rushed him and instinct won over the trickle of reason he had left in his body. In one swift motion, he swung, and every screaming emotion he'd been holding back exploded out through a closed fist against his brother's face.

Jude let out a cry of pent-up passion and Jonathan crumbled to the red-stained deck beneath their feet.

CHAPTER FORTY-FOUR

COMMANDER AADI

Vice Admiral Rohit had been Commander Aadi's leader for the entirety of his tenure. A couple decades his senior, Vice Admiral Rohit was in place as Gaon's military leader long before Commander Aadi ever picked up a blade. Aadi respected him. He idolized him. He spent most of his life trying to impress him; make him proud; and maybe, if he was truly successful, even earn a small portion of his respect.

Standing before him now, Commander Aadi's failures felt heavier than ever. The hope of one day measuring up in the eyes of his hero was ever escaping. Commander Aadi swallowed hard, unsure of what was coming.

Over the last few weeks, the Gaon militia had engaged several territories, leaving behind unforgettable damage in the least, irrevocable damage at best. Vice Admiral Rohit's objective was to disrupt. Gaon may not be big enough or strong enough to conquer all Physis, but they would make it hard for anyone who thought they could.

The Gaon name would be remembered—no matter what.

Since the day Commander Aadi returned, Vice Admiral Rohit had done nothing but ignore him. He may speak over a map or a strategy board, but he would not face the commander eye-to-eye. He didn't address him. He didn't turn toward him. He didn't confer with him.

Commander Aadi wasn't performing, and he knew it. And he knew the Vice Admiral knew it. The battles they engaged in since his return were all the same. His mind blurred, his voice was mute of commands, he made tactical errors, and worst of all, he had yet to swing his blade.

The mission to elevate Gaon used to fuel him and surge venom at anything that stood in his way. He desired to rise in rank, and to become as known as Vice Admiral Rohit was known, and to cause fear in anyone unlucky enough to see Gaon's colors fly into their horizon.

When word arrived that the Vice Admiral wanted to speak with him, Commander Aadi prepared for the worst. The time had finally come for him to face the consequences for his betrayal. He would take it like the soldier he was trained to be. He forced his shoulders back the last millimeter they would go, and he raised his chin in stoic silence. Vice Admiral Rohit stood with his back to the commander, watching the water through the small hole in the ship's wall. Without turning around, he asked Commander Aadi one question.

"Do you want to be here?"

Commander Aadi felt his shoulders fall at the question. His chin with them. His eyes broke their focus.

"Sir?" he stuttered in return.

The Vice Admiral turned and rested one hand behind his back while the other balled into a fist that pushed against the surface of the desk in front of him.

"It's a simple question," he said. "Answer it."

Stagnancy filled the cabin. Commander Aadi had expected to have to walk, to be demoted, to be charged with treason. He did not expect this question. He looked into the Vice Admiral's pure, dark eyes. They awaited his response unexcited and still, as a leader's. The silence was broken by a knock at the door and Commander Aadi breathed for the first time in a full minute.

"Vice Admiral, apologies. This is urgent."

The interrupting colonel stood at the door; his body alive with energy.

Vice Admiral Rohit nodded his acceptance of the interruption, and the colonel entered the cabin with two crewmen and a foreigner. Commander Aadi saw the reaction Vice Admiral Rohit tried to hide as the foreigner entered the room.

The foreigner was Agonian. There was no mistaking it. There, Gaon's greatest enemy stood, hat in hand, in the belly of their mother ship.

"You risk a lot coming here," the Vice Admiral said in a low, cautionary voice.

The man nodded feverishly.

"Yes sir, nearly shot out the water," the foreigner shot a derisive look at one of the crewmen.

"What news then?" the Vice Admiral replied, short and pointed.

The Agonian swallowed repeatedly, dipping his chin, and trying to gain his composure. His midnight skin shined with his efforts.

"Chief Issachar sails for the isles," he managed.

The Vice Admiral straightened. He looked to the colonel for confirmation and then back to the foreigner.

"You're certain?" he demanded.

The foreigner nodded in affirmation and explained, "Triton mutinied. Their fleet remains at the front. The isles are defenseless. Only Triton rabble remains."

Vice Admiral Rohit stared, captured by the foreigner's words. The foreigner swiped his hand across his slippery forehead, pushing sweat off and onto the wood below him.

"Chief Issachar sails for the isles with his warrior guard."

The Vice Admiral straightened his uniform down the front and sides.

"Your debt is paid, Akuji," he said to the foreigner. "You may go."

Commander Aadi watched the foreigner wither with the realization that he was free of whatever debt he owed while simultaneously imprisoned by the betrayal of what he'd exposed. The expression on the foreigner's face felt familiar. Like that of what Commander Aadi had seen in his own face. He wondered if Akuji would stand before the Agonian leader and pay for what he'd done. It would be easier than the purgatory in which Commander Aadi continued to exist.

The door closed behind the foreigner and pulled the commander back to the conversation he was having with the Vice Admiral before the interruption. His stomach jerked with newly set reality.

"Prepare your men," the Vice Admiral said.

The gravel in his voice set in deep.

"We're taking Agon."

CHAPTER FORTY-FIVE

JONATHAN

When Jonathan came to, Jude was sitting on the crimson-stained deck next to him. His back rested against the ship's wall and his knees bent up, holding his elbows. His face was dipped between his knees. The wildfire that blazed in Jude moments before was flickered out, and Jonathan was glad.

Jonathan squeezed his left eye against the pressure that was building there. He'd been unconscious long enough for it to swell, and now it was nearly closed shut. He touched it tenderly and righted himself against the wall next to his friend.

His stirring brought Jude's knees down and Jonathan watched him lay his head defeatedly against the wall of the ship behind him.

"Sorry," Jude said.

Jonathan didn't respond. After a long silence, Jude spoke again.

"I'm afraid."

Jonathan nodded his agreement. He'd felt it for the last two months. Not being able to share his fear with his brother had made it even more difficult. But telling Jude that now would only seem like an excuse, and it wasn't going to change anything.

"We have to go back," Jude said.

Jonathan nodded again at the air in front of him and chewed the inside of his mouth. He'd known it for a while. They should have turned back eight weeks ago. Hearing it said out loud was an immeasurable relief. He knew Collette wasn't going to like it, but it didn't matter. It's what had to be done.

"Is she okay?" Jude asked.

Jonathan turned his open eye toward Jude. Anxiety had found its place there again, and Jonathan knew it would remain until they set Collette on dry land. So often he'd found himself wanting what Jude had, but in this moment, he didn't envy it at all.

"Yeah," Jonathan said. "She's okay."

Jonathan knew any effort to instill calm in Jude would be wasted, so he didn't try. Apart from what Jude felt, the freedom to talk about the situation was going to ease Jonathan's burden immensely. It already had. He couldn't help but feel relieved.

Jude stood and offered him a hand. He helped Jonathan to his feet and embraced him. They tapped hands and wordlessly returned to their respective cabins with an old, familiar, shared goal—newly revived.

FOUR WEEKS LATER

The morning after their confrontation, Jonathan and Jude charted the path back to Zoar. Jude kept only enough people on board the Refuge to sail them home. He moved the rest of their crew to sister ships and ordered the fleet to stay in the effort, reinforcing the council's new rules and urging them to continue. Jonathan knew the council would not receive it well, but for he and Jude, there was no other choice. The Refuge took a hard left in course correction and raised her sails to full mast.

In the weeks since then, the Refuge's best efforts were not fast enough for Jude or Jonathan's comfort. With the battle-free days and only one goal, Jonathan found himself at the helm bending a friendly ear to Jude's process. His words rushed by as freely as the water they pushed through.

It was conflict unlike any other. Jude was torn between care for his family and the responsibilities he felt for the mission. In essence, he had two families to care for and they required different things. He found purpose in the mission. He knew he was made for it—he knew he was made to lead. It thrilled him, and he wanted it to succeed.

But Jude also found purpose in his household family. He knew he was made to protect and provide for them. He knew he was made to lead them. They thrilled him, and in an entirely different way. Visions of Josie teased him. He dreamt of her face, her smell, and the way her hair curled around her tiny face. He dreamt of her cackling laughter and the bounce that carried her.

Jude was the epitome of a torn man, and Jonathan could see it breaking him more with every day that passed.

Collette was no different.

Jonathan made it a point to put eyes on her daily, assessing the damage of the conflict and checking in on her physical health. The purple under her eyes remained a permanent fixture to her beautiful face, growing in depth and color over the past weeks. Her fatigue showed in her movements and her belly grew by the day, making the crew ever more aware of the clock that chased them. Whether she admitted it or not, Jonathan knew her physical condition was far from her biggest battle. Much more oppressive was the disruption of she and Jude's relationship.

And it wrecked the both of them.

When Jonathan stood at the helm, Jude stood next to him, either completely silent or a rushing fall that wouldn't be silenced. When Jonathan checked in on Collette, she unsettled him in new ways every day, disturbing him at her nearness to labor while devastating him with the pain in her expressions.

The Refuge was still an alarming distance from Zoar, but Jonathan knew they were already doing everything they could. His only job was to keep them on course, and that, he could do with his eyes closed.

He watched the noon sun sparkle life onto the passing water, and he let the warming breeze cover him. Collette stood against the starboard rail, rubbing her swollen belly, and periodically wiping tears from her eyes. As Jonathan watched her, he felt the weight of the discourse between she and Jude. It spoiled even the freshest ocean air.

Jonathan had loved Collette so much, for so long. He never would have guessed how much it would hurt him to see her at odds with Jude. He would have guessed it would feel more like a window, but it didn't. It felt like the bottom of a dried-out well. He watched her from across the deck thinking just how empty she looked. Without Jude, she was a shell without life— a home without people. Jude's love made her the Collette that Jonathan loved.

Together, Jude and Collette were light and poignancy. They were truth and tale. They were both daring and dutiful. Jonathan knew he would always love Collette. But for the first time, he realized he loved her most, because he loved Jude. And together, they were both better.

Suddenly, it felt easier.

Jude was easy to find. Jonathan approached him with intention, took the papers from under Jude's hands, and delivered his message as directly as he knew how.

"Fix it," he said.

He shook his head at Jude when he tried to talk, silencing any effort to refute him. It took a moment before Jude relinquished, but he did.

In watching his best friend walk toward reconciliation with the woman they both loved, Jonathan released what remained of his striving for her.

She wasn't his. She never was. And he didn't want her without Jude.

Jonathan returned to the helm and took the freest breath in his memory. He rested his eyes on the waters that would lead them home and fastened his gaze to a horizon he knew well.

CHAPTER FORTY-SIX

MATTHEW

The Diamond Isles

Readjusting to the bite in the breeze was easier than he thought it would be. Matthew's body embraced the climate to which it was most accustomed. For what felt like days, Matthew cleared debris away from the wreckage of the castle in solitude. The first man to appear at his side was one of the few remaining soldiers of the royal guard. The man said nothing but sauntered over to where Matthew worked and wordlessly began clearing rubble away with him.

Two weeks later, the group had grown seven strong. Their progress was slow, but it was progress. The act of it was more therapy than anything. There was a part of Matthew that wanted to see his childhood home restored, and wanted to see his father, the king, sleep in a proper bed again.

But the larger part of him didn't care much for the castle or for its restoration. The rebuilding wasn't about the castle at all—it was about Matthew. Labor had become his friend, and for the past few weeks, it was the only thing getting him through his newest nightmare.

He had no plan. He had no direction. He wasn't ready to be anything but numb. With each rising sun he only hungered to sweat and thirsted to ache with a good day's work.

Matthew would not allow himself to think of Kolpisi for fear of allowing himself the fantasy of a return. He could not, and would not, think about Faith's marriage to his father.

A dull grey soul to match the Diamond Isles sky was the only place he could exist for now, and he didn't know when that would change. Matthew didn't know how many estates he may have to rebuild until he could bear to process it all, but he would rebuild until he found the strength to look it all in the face. Even if he had to re-erect all the isles and Triton with them.

"Matthew."

He squeezed the muscles in his jaw to lessen his response. "I told you," he said dryly, "I go by Monroe now."

Faith put down the tray she carried with her. "And I told you," she said. "I'm not going to call you that."

Matthew didn't turn to look at her. He didn't need to. She would look the same as she had for the last two weeks. She would be dressed in an intricately detailed lace dress, too large for function and too delicate to do anything but sit foolishly still. She would have that look on her face—the one she wore every day since he'd walked into the hall—something akin to urgency, shame, and earnestness all at the same time.

He was tired of it. He was tired of the way it tempted him to feel.

The situation was disdainfully simple, and he didn't need her explanations or excuses. She couldn't wait for her chance to be queen. She could feign feelings for him and beg him to hear her side of the story, but there was no explaining this away. The one person who had made him feel like she wasn't after the crown, the one person for whom he was willing to return, the one person for whom he was willing to sacrifice his long-searched-for belonging—was the one person who had betrayed him.

He couldn't look at her. Looking at her was too generous.

She waited, like she did every day, turning pink in the cold, begging for his audience, but she eventually gave up. Just like every day previous.

At her adieu the men working beside Matthew offered their appropriate farewells, as was custom for a queen's departure, but Matthew wouldn't muster it. He didn't know if he ever would acknowledge the throne again. Certainly not while his father and Faith occupied it together. His father, the human-selling dictator who positioned one brand of human over all others. And Faith, who had deceived him, playing the part of an independent-minded companion when really, she targeted the throne like every other.

Matthew had planned to arrive home and tell his father off. He'd planned to righteously shout of the obscenities he'd seen and experienced. He dreamed about exposing his father to the residents of the isles and delivering one devastating truth after the other until the king was forced off the throne by his own royal guard.

But Triton had beaten him to it.

Triton would not be surpassed or outdone, and worse, they wouldn't be surprised by what Matthew had to say. They wouldn't step back aghast at the truth unveiled. They would likely yawn, and roll their eyes, and smirk at the ignorant, unrealized prince.

For all the truth he had to scream out, he had not one audience member at all. Triton need not be told. The isles were deserted, leaving nothing but the empty remains of once-glorious estates. And then there was Faith, with whom he was the most anxious to share, but he wouldn't be sharing much more than a cursory glance with her. He couldn't help but question his choice to return. He'd come at her bidding because she called for help.

But by the looks of it, she'd found all the help she needed, herself.

Matthew stopped working and looked out across the water from which he'd come. Then, he let his eyes fall to the rubble underneath him. One people to whom he belonged but who didn't know him. Another people who knew every scrap of his ugly truth, but to whom he did not belong.

He considered his options.

The silence that answered him turned him back to the task of clearing away the mess under his feet. What else was there to do? What option existed?

He rubbed the stubble of his shaved head and then bent to lift another mass of rock from the wreckage.

ONE WEEK LATER

The appeals from Faith didn't stop. Day after day she returned, but Matthew didn't budge in his resolve.

A few members of the royal guard were uncomfortable at Matthew's willingness to openly disrespect their new queen, but it didn't stop them from helping him. They grunted their awkwardness or adjusted their posture when she walked by, but it didn't move Matthew.

They could all take a knee if they wanted. He wouldn't budge.

He wished he could give them that kind of freedom, but it wasn't the kind that could be gifted. It was something for which one would have to bleed. As he had.

The wind came in from the water and set red into his fingers and face. He could feel the cold tightening his skin and he moved against it to keep warm. Down the walkway, the approaching rattle of a tray combined with the click-clack of heels told him who was arriving.

She was early today.

"It's starting to look like home again," she said, squinting into the wind.

"Whose home?" Matthew asked.

She chuckled. "Well, yours, of course."

He turned from her to continue his work. "Not my home," he said dryly.

"Then why do you work to restore it?" she quipped.

Two of the men helped as they worked a large piece of wall back into place. When it landed where it should, Matthew turned to her, and in between heavy breaths he answered.

"I don't know," he said.

Matthew pivoted to the next pile of waiting rubble, using his every effort to ignore her. She started in on her typical pleas, but Matthew had become proficient at shutting it out. She waited for a few moments, and then turned on her heel to approach one of the royal guards. He was the first to join Matthew those weeks ago, and he'd worked by his side since then.

Faith spoke a few indistinct words to the guard before turning to Matthew.

"Matthew, I know you don't want to hear from me, you've made that much clear. But this isn't about me—it's about all of us. Please," Faith said.

Matthew didn't stop working but he eyed the guard to whom she'd spoken. The man caught Matthew's look and gave him a slight nod. His eyes were stern, cautionary. It was enough for Matthew to offer her a slightly raised attention. He shrugged his shoulders and kept working.

"If you must..." he said, exasperated.

"I wonder if we could step away in private?" Faith asked.

"No," he said sharply, "if you want to speak, speak."

He noticed how Faith glanced around at the guards working near enough to hear her. If it was important enough, she would say it front of them. She proceeded awkwardly, trying to whisper over the waves unsuccessfully.

"The king has maintained his meetings with the high officials who remain loyal to him, and I attended the meeting yesterday."

Matthew raised an eyebrow at the thought of the queen attending one of his father's meetings. His mother never would have had the gall to ask, but he shouldn't be surprised that Faith did. He wondered what agenda she may have had in mind with a move like that.

Faith paused before continuing, glancing around at the other men again, clearly uncomfortable at speaking in front of them.

"Matthew, our fleet at the warfront, they have not been informed of the mutiny."

At this, all the men within earshot stopped working—including Matthew.

Faith continued, "Helodias tried to convince your father that they must be informed and return. You know how vulnerable we are with no guard here." Concern spread across Faith's face. "Matthew, you know when other territories find out we've been overthrown, they will come with all they have to take what's left." Her voice broke with emotion. "Our greatest threat has never been Triton. Others will not be so merciful."

She was right.

Triton left some of the castle, but more importantly, they left people alive. No foreign territory would have that kind of mercy. Although Matthew didn't grieve the loss of Diamond Isles rule, or what it stood for, he was reminded of what he sacrificed when he left.

He could have changed it all without bloodshed, without the mutiny, and without the devastation under his feet. He didn't want to see another territory add annihilation to what was already a pile of ruins.

Matthew assumed the Diamond Isles fleet knew. He

assumed everyone knew. He assumed the isles had no militia left—that they'd already been called home to protect their own walls.

The news should have spread over all Physis. It should have been the biggest story for anyone who had ears, and when people found out, it would be—and every territory in Physis would sail to take the once-unquestioned authority for all it had left.

Purpose relit in Matthew like a dry leaf in a fire.

The stone he held fell and shattered into pieces while he strode toward his father's study for the first time in over two years.

CHAPTER FORTY-SEVEN

JONAS

Jonas' mind oozed with the satisfaction he felt when Issachar told him to remain behind. He would finally have his rightful place as the Chief of Agon. It was a position he earned long ago. He would savor it, and he would use the opportunity to prove to the people of Agon that he was their rightful leader.

Discontent was as high as it had ever been in their land. The early deployment shook long-time loyalists from Issachar's hold, and then he sailed away for an offensive attack while his people were at their most vulnerable.

He knew if he waited long enough, Issachar would misstep, and it finally happened.

Jonas was chief now. All he had to do was survive the battle.

He dipped to miss the swing that came at his head and thrust his sword into the man who delivered it. The man crumbled to the ground in front of him and he removed his sword and readied for the next.

COMMANDER AADI

Commander Aadi tried to coax adrenaline into his veins as the Gaon troops covered the residential lanes of Agon. He ran, surrounded by his men who plowed through anything standing and slashed through anything that breathed.

Agonian screams filled the air. The sound that once flushed Commander Aadi with energy now slowed him like sand-filled boots. He lifted his blade time after time, but it was much hungrier than he was.

By the time he reached the main bunker, his weapon shined as cleanly as it did when they dropped anchor. His blade gleaned off the sun and into his eyes, shaming him, while he and his unit made their way through the arena and into the chief's residence.

Alarms sounded over the land, muting their communication down to hand signals.

Not that they needed them. They all knew what to do. They all knew who they hunted. Commander Aadi hoped he could do what they were sent to do.

If not, he would not survive another day in the in between.

AMORA

A sickening feeling came over Amora the moment her husband announced his departure. In her lifetime, the chief of Agon had never left their land. It was the chief's duty to stay— to protect. It was the Agonian way.

She didn't understand how this could happen. She should have said more. She should have urged him to stay. She should have listened to the feeling in her gut. He always told her to.

When the alarms sounded, she rushed the girls into acquiescence. They'd ignored the bells so many times, but everything was different lately.

Eden too.

Eden's indifference to Agonian tradition made Amora uneasy. If her eldest child was willing to rebel against two-hundred-year-old custom, where would it stop? What else would she be willing to do if Agon tradition wasn't a code by which she would live? The possibilities were frightening.

After Issachar sent Amafis away and put an end to Eden's war training, the fires that lived under Eden's skin simmered down to a glow that seemed to have gone out completely. It was hard to watch her daughter go through the pain, but Amora knew it was the best thing for her. Even if it made her for a time, a little lifeless.

And then the bells rang.

When the alarms sounded and the screams started, excitement rushed over Eden like a tsunami. It set her aflame. She rushed around and gathered everyone in the barracks, corralling them like chicks in a pen, commanding them with clarity and authority.

Amora sensed the urgency in her daughter and affirmed her directions to the others until everyone in the chief's estate was safely inside the bunker.

And then, when she expected Eden to lock the door behind them, she pushed Amora in, closed the door, and locked herself out.

EDEN

Eden rushed directly for the arena and armed herself with as many of her father's remaining weapons she could agilely carry. Everyone was locked away and safe. That's all she needed to know.

She couldn't hear her mother's scream after she shut the door, but she knew it came. She didn't need to imagine what it sounded like. The color drained out of her face and panic overtook her eyes, but Eden didn't have time for apologies. Agon needed help, and with her father away, every sword would matter.

The beat of her heart was heavy and strong, and it carried all the way through her chest and down into her arms, raising every strike in rhythm with her stride. This is what it was to be Agonian. The thrill of it was nearly more than she could bear; it electrified her. She didn't let her mind think over what was happening, she just let her training take her for all she was, accepting each attack as it came.

She moved down the corridor fighting as she went until a blow to the chest knocked her backward and her head hit the unforgiving clay beneath her. She moaned and rolled to the side to regain her weapon just as the glimmer of a clean, silver blade whooshed through the air and moved in directly under her chin.

ISSACHAR

Issachar leaned over the side of the deck, slave to the sea sickness that wrecked him. He'd spent most of his life with his feet on solid ground. He knew his body wasn't keen to the sea, but this was a misery unforeseen. The battle awaiting him in the isles would be the most important battle of his life. But that fact wasn't salve enough for the burn he felt leaving Agon behind... leaving his girls behind.

They were vulnerable. Regardless of the opportunity, it was an unsettling time to leave. Nothing felt as it should. His unease was not just sea sickness, and he knew it. He lifted his eyes to the horizon and prayed for relief. The Diamond Isles would be within reach in just a few more weeks.

And then, this would all be worth it. He hoped.

KING OF THE DIAMOND ISLES

King of the Ashes.

That's what they called him when they broke through the walls.

All his life he upheld the standards of the great kings of the isles before him. He did everything he could to keep Physis in their control. What did it earn him? A broken kingdom, a son who hated him, and his one light; his queen; his great love; taken from him by a disease the healers could not name. How to avenge the death of a loved one against a disease? It would haunt him until the day he died. It was a day for which he yearned.

"There's a moment in which every great king must lay his cards on the table and accept his defeat," his father used to tell him. "That is the day he becomes great."

He never agreed with it. He still didn't.

Matthew urged him to send word to the fleet that they'd been conquered by their own—Triton. Although it was satisfying to see his son finally show interest in protecting the kingdom, the king saw no point in it now. It was too little, too late. Let them run out of resources on the warfront. Let them die out there. At least they would die believing they fought for a victorious kingdom, not the wasted glory that lay before him.

Word would spread, and the lot of Physis would sail to conquer the great Diamond Isles. He'd made enough enemies over the years to make it a race for who could arrive first.

No, he would not send word of their defeat.

The Diamond Isles fleet remaining on the warfront would

be the last to remember him as a great king. A successful king. The king of diamonds, not ashes.

MATTHEW

The blasts came in fast and unseen. The barriers they had built over the last few weeks survived two rounds from the hungry Agonian warships before they crumbled with what was left of the castle. When the explosions finally subsided, Matthew waded through the remains, searching for life and hoping to find the king and queen—despite his feelings toward them.

He found Faith quickly; a royal guard had tucked her safely away in the bunker during the attack. It took much longer to find the king, who true to form, had obstinately waited out the blasts seated righteously on his throne.

Matthew knew his father. He would have said it was a noble act to fall with his kingdom.

But Matthew wasn't going to call it that. It wasn't noble, it was cowardice. It was a man unwilling to do the harder thing and *live*. It was a man unwilling to look his own mistakes in the eye. A man unwilling to correct them.

Matthew found the king in the rubble, under a pile of rock, suffocating in what he spent his life worshiping. Matthew removed what he could and knelt next to him, knowing it was his father's end. Matthew pitied him for the power he so desperately clung to. It couldn't save him now. Nothing could.

Matthew remained next to the king long after his chest ceased filling with air. He stared into his father's face, but it held no more peace in its death than it did in its life.

Matthew didn't feel the grief he'd felt at his mother's death. He felt paralyzed.

No king. No isles. No home.

The devastation he sat in was the very picture of his life.

Every figurative or literal effort to rebuild it over the last two years had been left behind in Kolpisi or blown away with the castle that lay in crumbles around him.

Faith found him eventually. She didn't say anything. She just came as close as she could and dropped a letter on the rock nearest him. It had his name on the front, written in her own, familiar hand.

Matthew,

A lot changed when you left, but I didn't. I never cared to be queen; and you know that. But my preferences ceased to matter the day Triton ships landed in the isles. When overthrow was imminent, my parents and Hodes rushed me to the castle and begged the king to take me.

And by some miracle, he did. We were hidden together in the bunker and tediously joined by a guard. I don't even know if it was legal, but it was the only way to legitimize my being spared when no one else was. And it was the only part of the union in which we participated.

I don't think he saved me for his own pleasure or satisfaction, Matthew. I think he saved me for you.

I found a picture. It's enclosed here. Take a careful look.

I asked him about it, but he only offered silence. It was the old housemaid, the one who served your mother, who finally answered my question.

It's your radiant mother there, holding those two beautiful babies. The housemaid said you knew you were a twin, but that your sister died in childbirth. Well, she didn't. There she is, next to you on your mother's lap, bright and beautiful and alive.

Why did they tell you she died, I wondered? All the housemaid was willing to tell me was that the answer was in the picture. Although annoyed at her vagueness, I spent time with the photo, searching it for a clue, for some reason for the deceit.

And that's when I found it.

Look at your sister's eyes. Look at her hair. Look at the structure of her face. It's hard to tell on an infant, but it would have become very obvious, very quickly.

She's recessive, Matthew. I don't know why, and I don't know how, but somewhere in your family, there's mixed blood. And if there was mixed blood in your line, it would have illegitimated your father's title. All of you would've been excommunicated to Triton—at best.

When I asked the housemaid about it, she wouldn't confirm it, but she took the photo from me, and she wrote on the back.

I think it's just what you need. It may be what we all need.

Love,
Faith

Matthew took the photo and carefully examined it. Everything Faith explained was plainly observable. Big, dark eyes stared at him from the photo. The baby was beautiful, but she was not pure.

He turned the photo over and saw words written in his mother's beautiful script handwriting. The sight of her familiar hand made him smile.

"MOTHER, MATTHEW, AND COLLETTE"

At the bottom of the photo, scribbled in fresh ink and in the foreign hand of the old housemaid, was the same, resilient word that had chased him since the day his mother died.

"ZOAR"

EPILOGUE

The Physis Sea

One of Jonathan's tattooed hands rested on the helm of the Refuge in a well-worn groove. He stood with the other hand in his pocket, his eyes fixed to the horizon, watching it like it was his soul itself. The western breeze brought with it the smell of rain, and he inhaled it deeply, anticipating the cleanse of the coming shower.

Footsteps approached from behind him, not surprising him in the least. He'd seen it coming for days, and he was looking forward to it. He didn't turn to face the order when it came.

"North, Jonathan," she said.

He smiled.

"Ay, ay, Captain."

He finished working the wheel in its new direction, and felt a familiar hand drop gently on to his shoulder.

Familiar, but not the same. Never quite the same.

"Zoar," she said with anticipation.

"Home, Josie," Jonathan said. "We're going home."

ACKNOWLEDGMENTS

What is ever accomplished alone? I'm not sure anything is. I'm certain this was not.

To the tribe: On this Earth I will never know why we got the gift of each other, but I'll never stop being thankful for it, and for each one of you. Gary and Michele, your blistered hands and sunburnt backs laid the very bricks I walk upon. Our lives are rich because of your mission, and every one of us knows it - and so will the next generation, and the next, and the next. Thank you for your unwavering commitment to that mission, and to us. Seth, Coley, Erin, Phil, and Kenan, each one of you has come alongside and loved and supported and encouraged me and this project in various ways. Sometimes it was hard. Sometimes it was sweet. It was always strengthening. Thank you. And to Carolyn, who I am so thankful I have come to know and love as an adult. You are a grandmother, yes, and you are also a treasured friend. Your support along the way has been invaluable.

To the Mills Market staff: you may prefer Samson to me, but you served us graciously, patiently, and with enduring kindness. Thank you all.

To the longest journeyer, Cortlan, whose friendship cannot be captured by a set of words on a page. I stopped counting at twenty years, and for both our sakes, let's not worry about the number anymore. Each one of your missions is singularly focused on lifting other people; providing roads to the world for the untraveled; and normalizing success for anyone who can dream it up. This is for you too, as one who encouraged me to write before I knew I had words to give.

To the people who helped me carry on: the early readers. You are crucial to the process, and you put up with the junk. Overwritten sentences, too many details, typos, and iffy story lines. You stuck with it and provided feedback and told me where I was off and where I was nearly getting it. If this project has any merit at all, it's in no small part credited to your collective value.

And to Justin, who was not an early reader but played perhaps the most vital role of all – that of accountability. You are the singular force who was willing to tick me off to hold me accountable. You are invaluable.

And finally, to my nieces and nephews, whose names, personalities, and characters are all over this project. You inspire me by the ways you learn and love. I hope you stay curious; I pray you always push beyond how culture will inform you; and I challenge you to never, never, never be afraid to fall. Because that, my darlings, is how you will learn to fly. It hurts; but it's worth every scar if it gets you off the ground every now and again. I love you each one.

ABOUT ATMOSPHERE PRESS

Atmosphere Press is an independent, full-service publisher for excellent books in all genres and for all audiences. Learn more about what we do at atmospherepress.com.

We encourage you to check out some of Atmosphere's latest releases, which are available at Amazon.com and via order from your local bookstore:

Twisted Silver Spoons, a novel by Karen M. Wicks

Queen of Crows, a novel by S.L. Wilton

The Summer Festival is Murder, a novel by Jill M. Lyon

The Past We Step Into, stories by Richard Scharine

Swimming with the Angels, a novel by Colin Kersey

Island of Dead Gods, a novel by Verena Mahlow

Cloakers, a novel by Alexandra Lapointe

Twins Daze, a novel by Jerry Petersen

Embargo on Hope, a novel by Justin Doyle

Abaddon Illusion, a novel by Lindsey Bakken

Blackland: A Utopian Novel, by Richard A. Jones

The Embers of Tradition, a novel by Chukwudum Okeke

Saints and Martyrs: A Novel, by Aaron Roe

When I Am Ashes, a novel by Amber Rose

The Recoleta Stories, by Bryon Esmond Butler

Voodoo Hideaway, a novel by Vance Cariaga

Hart Street and Main, a novel by Tabitha Sprunger

The Weed Lady, a novel by Shea R. Embry

A Book of Life, a novel by David Ellis

It Was Called a Home, a novel by Brian Nisun

Grace, a novel by Nancy Allen

ABOUT THE AUTHOR

N. Ford spends free time in the open air, usually barefooted and with readily available mango. With the steady company of a giant dog and something to write on, anywhere will do. Defined by faith, fueled by tribe, and driven by purpose, N. Ford writes for all; and simultaneously, for just One.

Kindly leave your review:

Amazon

Goodreads

Barnes & Noble

Socials

Read on for an excerpt from N. Ford's next novel

BOOK TWO OF THE REFUGE TRILOGY:
REFUGE RED

CHAPTER ONE

JOSIE

Present - The Physis Sea

Josie walked the deck as she did every morning, the ship more her home than any other. She embraced its dips and sways with settled familiarity and ceaseless craving. She worked her father's list, pushing the wrinkled paper against its clipboard when it lifted in the wind. She checked the lay of each board, the drape of each mast, the wear of every rope. She scanned the horizon and marked off crew at every post.

Josie remembered the day Jonathan had lifted the clipboard off its rusted nail and placed it in her hands for the first time. She remembered his reserved smile and the deliberate way he breathed. Jonathan had always been the source of steady composure in her life, but the expression he wore that day wasn't born of calm. It was quiet, sure, but it was also conflicted.

Josie didn't have to ask Jonathan why his forehead pinched the way it did. She knew why his eyes wouldn't lift to hers. Some days, she felt like she knew the conflict that lived in Jonathan better than he knew it himself. But she wasn't going to let it stop her. She simply smiled in knowing resolve and lifted the clipboard lightly, right out of his hands....